RICHARD BRAUTIGAN'S BOOKS

REVENGE
of the
Lawn

STORIES
1962-1970
BY RICHARD BRAUTIGAN

A *Touchstone Book* - Simon and Schuster - *New York*

Some of these stories first appeared in *Rolling Stone, Playboy, Ramparts, New American Review, Vogue, Coyote's Journal, Mademoiselle, Nice, Tri-Quarterly, Esquire, Evergreen Review, Kulchur, Now Now, Sum, Jeopardy, R. C. Lion, Parallel,* and *Change.*

Copyright © 1963, 1964, 1965, 1966,
1967, 1969, 1970, 1971
by Richard Brautigan
Published by Simon and Schuster
Rockefeller Center, 630 Fifth Avenue
New York, New York 10020
First printing
SBN 671-20960-4 Casebound edition
SBN 671-20961-2 Touchstone paperback edition
Library of Congress Catalog Card Number: 76-154094
Designed by Grabhorn-Hoyem, San Francisco
Manufactured in the United States of America
Photography by Edmund Shea

This book is for
Don Carpenter

CONTAINING:

REVENGE OF
THE LAWN

My grandmother, in her own way, shines like a beacon down the stormy American past. She was a bootlegger in a little county up in the state of Washington. She was also a handsome woman, close to six feet tall who carried 190 pounds in the grand operatic manner of the early 1900s. And her specialty was bourbon, a little raw but a welcomed refreshment in those Volstead Act days.

She of course was no female Al Capone, but her bootlegging feats were the cornucopia of legend in her neck of the woods, as they say. She had the county in her pocket for years. The sheriff used to call her up every morning and give her the weather report and tell her how the chickens were laying.

I can imagine her talking to the sheriff: "Well, Sheriff, I hope your mother gets better soon. I had a cold and a bad sore throat last week myself. I've still got the sniffles. Tell her hello for me and to drop by the next time she's down this way. And if you want that case, you can pick it up or I can have it sent over as soon as Jack gets back with the car."

"No, I don't know if I'm going to the firemen's ball this year, but you know that my heart is with the firemen. If you don't see me there tonight, you tell the boys that. No, I'll try to get there, but I'm still not fully recovered from my cold. It kind of climbs on me in the evening."

My grandmother lived in a three-story house that was old even in those days. There was a pear tree in the front yard which was heavily eroded by rain from years of not having any lawn.

The picket fence that once enclosed the lawn was gone, too, and people just drove their cars right up to the porch. In the winter the front yard was a mud hole and in the summer it was hard as a rock.

Jack used to curse the front yard as if it were a living thing. He was the man who lived with my grandmother for thirty years. He was not my grandfather, but an Italian who came down the road one day selling lots in Florida.

He was selling a vision of eternal oranges and sunshine door to door in a land where people ate apples and it rained a lot.

Jack stopped at my grandmother's house to sell her a lot just a stone's throw from downtown Miami, and he was delivering her whiskey a week later. He stayed for thirty years and Florida went on without him.

Jack hated the front yard because he thought it was against him. There had been a beautiful lawn there when Jack came along, but he let it wander off into nothing. He refused to water it or take care of it in any way.

Now the ground was so hard that it gave his car flat tires in the summer. The yard was always finding a nail to put in one of his tires or the car was always sinking out of sight in the winter when the rains came on.

The lawn had belonged to my grandfather who lived out the end of his life in an insane asylum. It had been his pride and joy and was said to be the place where his powers came from.

My grandfather was a minor Washington mystic who in 1911 prophesied the exact date when World War I would start: June 28, 1914, but it had been too much for him. He never got to enjoy the fruit of his labor because they had to put him away in 1913 and he spent seventeen years in the state insane asylum believing he was a child and it was actually May 3, 1872.

He believed that he was six years old and it was a cloudy day about to rain and his mother was baking a chocolate cake. It stayed May 3, 1872 for my grandfather until he died in 1930. It took seventeen years for that chocolate cake to be baked.

There was a photograph of my grandfather. I look a great deal like him. The only difference being that I am over six feet tall and he was not quite five feet tall. He had a dark idea that being so short, so close to the earth and his lawn would help to prophesy the exact date when World War I would start.

It was a shame that the war started without him. If only he could have held back his childhood for another year, avoided that chocolate cake, all of his dreams would have come true.

There were always two large dents in my grandmother's house that had never been repaired and one of them came about this way: In the autumn the pears would get ripe on the tree in the front yard and the pears would fall on the ground and rot and bees would gather by the hundreds to swarm on them.

The bees somewhere along the line had picked up the habit of stinging Jack two or three times a year. They would sting him in the most ingenious ways.

Once a bee got in his wallet and he went down to the store to buy some food for dinner, not knowing the mischief that he carried in his pocket.

He took out his wallet to pay for the food.

"That will be 72 cents," the grocer said.

"AAAAAAAAAAAAAAAAAAAAAAAAA!" Jack replied, looking down to see a bee busy stinging him on the little finger.

The first large dent in the house was brought about by still another bee landing on Jack's cigar as he was driving the car into the front yard that peary autumn the stock market crashed.

The bee ran down the cigar, Jack could only stare at it cross-eyed in terror, and stung him on the upper lip. His reaction to this was to drive the car immediately into the house.

That front yard had quite a history after Jack let the lawn go to hell. One day in 1932 Jack was off running an errand or delivering something for my grandmother. She wanted to dump the old mash and get a new batch going.

Because Jack was gone, she decided to do it herself. Grandmother put on a pair of railroad overalls that she used for working around the still and filled a wheelbarrow with mash and dumped it out in the front yard.

She had a flock of snow-white geese that roamed outside the house and nested in the garage that had not been used to park the car since the time Jack had come along selling futures in Florida.

Jack had some kind of idea that it was all wrong for a car to have a house. I think it was something that he had learned in the Old Country. The answer was in Italian because that was the only language Jack used when he talked about the garage. For everything else he used English, but it was only Italian for the garage.

After Grandmother had dumped the mash on the ground near the pear tree, she went back to the still down in the basement and the geese all gathered around the mash and started talking it over.

I guess they came to a mutually agreeable decision because they all started eating the mash. As they ate the mash their eyes got brighter and brighter and their voices, in appreciation of the mash, got louder and louder.

After a while one of the geese stuck his head in the mash and forgot to take it out. Another one of the geese cackled madly and tried to stand on one leg and give a W. C. Fields imitation of a stork. He maintained that position for about a minute before he fell on his tail feathers.

My grandmother found them all lying around the mash in the positions that they had fallen. They looked as if they had been machine-gunned. From the height of her operatic splendor she thought they were all dead.

She responded to this by plucking all their feathers and piling their bald bodies in the wheelbarrow and wheeling them down to the basement. She had to make five trips to accommodate them.

She stacked them like cordwood near the still and waited for Jack to return and dispose of them in a way that would provide a goose for dinner and a small profit by selling the rest of the flock in town. She went upstairs to take a nap after finishing with the still.

It was about an hour later that the geese woke up. They had devastating hangovers. They had all kind of gathered themselves uselessly to their feet when suddenly one of the geese noticed that he did not have any feathers. He informed the other geese of their condition, too. They were all in despair.

They paraded out of the basement in a forlorn and wobbly gang. They were all standing in a cluster near the pear tree when Jack drove into the front yard.

The memory of the time he had been stung on the mouth by that bee must have come back to his mind when he saw the defeathered geese standing there, because suddenly like a madman he tore out the cigar he had stuck in his mouth and threw it away from him as hard as he could. This caused his hand to travel through the windshield. A feat that cost him thirty-two stitches.

The geese stood by staring on like some helpless, primitive American advertisement for aspirin under the pear tree as Jack drove his car into the house for the second and last time in the Twentieth Century.

★   ★   ★

The first time I remember anything in life occurred in my grandmother's front yard. The year was either 1936 or 1937. I remember a man, probably Jack, cutting down the pear tree and soaking it with kerosene.

It looked strange, even for a first memory of life, to watch a man pour gallons and gallons of kerosene all over a tree lying stretched out thirty feet or so on the ground, and then to set fire to it while the fruit was still green on the branches.

1692 COTTON MATHER
NEWSREEL

O 1939 Tacoma Washington witch, where are you now that
I am growing toward you? Once my body occupied a child's
space and doors had a large meaning to them and were almost
human. Opening a door meant something in 1939 and the
children used to make fun of you because you were crazy
and lived by yourself in an attic across the street from where
we sat in the gutter like two slum sparrows.

We were four years old.

I think you were about as old as I am now with the children
always teasing and calling after you, "The crazy woman!
Run! Run! The witch! The witch! Don't let her look at you in
the eye. She looked at me! Run! Help! Run!"

Now I am beginning to look like you with my long hippie
hair and my strange clothes. I look about as crazy in 1967
as you did in 1939.

Little children yell, "Hey, hippie!" at me in the San
Francisco mornings like we yelled, "Hey, crazy woman!" at
you plodding through Tacoma twilights.

I guess you got used to it as I've gotten used to it.

As a child I would always hang my hat on a dare. Dare me to do anything and I'd do it. Ugh! some of the things that I did following, like a midget Don Quixote, trails and visions of dares.

We were sitting in the gutter doing nothing. Perhaps we were waiting for the witch or anything to happen that would free us from the gutter. We had been sitting there for almost an hour: child's time.

"I dare you to go up to the witch's house and wave at me out the window," my friend said, finally to get things going.

I looked up at the witch's house across the street. There was one window in her attic facing down upon us like a still photograph from a horror movie.

"OK," I said.

"You've got guts," my friend said. I can't remember his name now. The decades have filed it off my memory, leaving a small empty place where his name should be.

I got up from the gutter and walked across the street and around to the back of the house where the stairs were that led to her attic. They were gray wooden stairs like an old mother cat and went up three flights to her door.

There were some garbage cans at the bottom of the stairs. I wondered what garbage can was the witch's. I lifted up one garbage can lid and looked inside to see if there was any witches' garbage in the can.

There wasn't.

The can was filled with just ordinary garbage. I lifted up the lid to the next garbage can but there wasn't any witches' garbage in that can either. I tried the third can but it was the same as the other two cans: no witches' garbage.

There were three garbage cans and there were three apartments in the house, including the attic where she lived. One of the cans had to be her garbage but there wasn't any difference between her garbage and the other people's garbage.

   . . . so . . .

I walked up the stairs to the attic. I walked very carefully as if I were petting an old gray mother cat nursing her kittens.

I finally arrived at the witch's door. I didn't know whether she was inside or not. She could have been home. I felt like knocking but that didn't make any sense. If she were there, she'd just slam the door in my face or ask me what I wanted and I'd run screaming down the stairs, "Help! Help! She looked at me!"

The door was tall, silent and human like a middle-aged woman. I felt as if I were touching her hand when I opened the door delicately like the inside of a watch.

The first room in the house was her kitchen and she wasn't in it, but there were twenty or thirty vases and jars and bottles filled with flowers. They were on the kitchen table and on all the shelves and ledges. Some of the flowers were stale and some of the flowers were fresh.

I went inside the next room and it was the living room and she wasn't there either, but again there were twenty or thirty vases and jars and bottles filled with flowers.

The flowers made my heart beat faster.

Her garbage had lied to me.

I went inside the last room and it was her bedroom and she wasn't there either, but again the twenty or thirty vases and jars and bottles filled with flowers.

There was a window right next to the bed and it was the window that looked down on the street. The bed was made of brass with a patchwork quilt on it. I walked over to the window and stood there staring down at my friend who was sitting in the gutter looking up at the window.

He couldn't believe that I was standing there in the witch's window and I waved very slowly at him and he waved very slowly at me. Our waving seemed to be very distant travelling from our arms like two people waving at each other in different cities, perhaps between Tacoma and Salem, and our waving was merely an echo of their waving across thousands of miles.

Now the dare had been completed and I turned around in that house which was like a shallow garden and all my fears collapsed upon me like a landslide of flowers and I ran screaming at the top of my lungs outside and down the stairs. I sounded as if I had stepped in a wheelbarrow-sized pile of steaming dragon shit.

When I came screaming around the side of the house, my friend jumped up from the gutter and started screaming, too. I guess he thought that the witch was chasing me. We ran screaming through the streets of Tacoma, pursued by our own voices like a 1692 Cotton Mather newsreel.

This was a month or two before the German Army marched into Poland.

1/3, 1/3, 1/3

It was all to be done in thirds. I was to get 1/3 for doing the typing, and she was to get 1/3 for doing the editing, and he was to get 1/3 for writing the novel.

We were going to divide the royalties three ways. We all shook hands on the deal, each knowing what we were supposed to do, the path before us, the gate at the end.

I was made a 1/3 partner because I had the typewriter.

I lived in a cardboard-lined shack of my own building across the street from the run-down old house the Welfare rented for her and her nine-year-old son Freddy.

The novelist lived in a trailer a mile away beside a sawmill pond where he was the watchman for the mill.

I was about seventeen and made lonely and strange by that Pacific Northwest of so many years ago, that dark, rainy land of 1952. I'm thirty-one now and I still can't figure out what I meant by living the way I did in those days.

She was one of those eternally fragile women in their late thirties and once very pretty and the object of much attention in the roadhouses and beer parlors, who are now on Welfare and their entire lives rotate around that one day a month when they get their Welfare checks.

The word "check" is the one religious word in their lives, so they always manage to use it at least three or four times in every conversation. It doesn't matter what you are talking about.

The novelist was in his late forties, tall, reddish, and looked as if life had given him an endless stream of two-timing girl-friends, five-day drunks and cars with bad transmissions.

He was writing the novel because he wanted to tell a story that had happened to him years before when he was working in the woods.

He also wanted to make some money: 1/3.

My entrance into the thing came about this way: One day I was standing in front of my shack, eating an apple and staring at a black ragged toothache sky that was about to rain.

What I was doing was like an occupation for me. I was that involved in looking at the sky and eating the apple. You would have thought that I had been hired to do it with a good salary and a pension if I stared at the sky long enough.

"HEY, YOU!" I heard somebody yell.

I looked across the mud puddle and it was the woman. She was wearing a kind of green Mackinaw that she wore all the time, except when she had to visit the Welfare people downtown. Then she put on a shapeless duck-gray coat.

We lived in a poor part of town where the streets weren't paved. The street was nothing more than a big mud puddle that you had to walk around. The street was of no use to cars any more. They travelled on a different frequency where asphalt and gravel were more sympathetic.

She was wearing a pair of white rubber boots that she

always had on in the winter, a pair of boots that gave her a kind of child-like appearance. She was so fragile and firmly indebted to the Welfare Department that she often looked like a child twelve years old.

"What do you want?" I said.

"You have a typewriter, don't you?" she said. "I've walked by your shack and heard you typing. You type a lot at night."

"Yeah, I have a typewriter," I said.

"You a good typist?" she said.

"I'm all right."

"We don't have a typewriter. How would you like to go in with us?" she yelled across the mud puddle. She looked a perfect twelve years old, standing there in her white boots, the sweetheart and darling of all mud puddles.

"What's 'go in' mean?"

"Well, he's writing a novel," she said. "He's good. I'm editing it. I've read a lot of pocketbooks and the *Reader's Digest*. We need somebody who has a typewriter to type it up. You'll get 1/3. How does that sound?"

"I'd like to see the novel," I said. I didn't know what was happening. I knew she had three or four boyfriends that were always visiting her.

"Sure!" she yelled. "You have to see it to type it. Come on around. Let's go out to his place right now and you can meet him and have a look at the novel. He's a good guy. It's a wonderful book."

"OK," I said, and walked around the mud puddle to where she was standing in front of her evil dentist house, twelve years old, and approximately two miles from the Welfare office.

"Let's go," she said.

★   ★   ★

We walked over to the highway and down the highway past mud puddles and sawmill ponds and fields flooded with rain until we came to a road that went across the railroad tracks and turned down past half a dozen small sawmill ponds that were filled with black winter logs.

We talked very little and that was only about her check that was two days late and she had called the Welfare and they said they mailed the check and it should be there tomorrow, but call again tomorrow if it's not there and we'll prepare an emergency money order for you.

"Well, I hope it's there tomorrow," I said.

"So do I or I'll have to go downtown," she said.

Next to the last sawmill pond was a yellow old trailer up on blocks of wood. One look at that trailer showed that it was never going anywhere again, that the highway was in distant heaven, only to be prayed to. It was really sad with a cemetery-like chimney swirling jagged dead smoke in the air above it.

A kind of half-dog, half-cat creature was sitting on a rough plank porch that was in front of the door. The creature half-barked and half-meowed at us, "Arfeow!" and darted under the trailer, looking out at us from behind a block.

"This is it," the woman said.

The door to the trailer opened and a man stepped out onto the porch. There was a pile of firewood stacked on the porch and it was covered with a black tarp.

The man held his hand above his eyes, shielding his eyes from a bright imaginary sun, though everything had turned dark in anticipation of the rain.

"Hello, there," he said.

"Hi," I said.

"Hello, honey," she said.

He shook my hand and welcomed me to his trailer, then

he gave her a little kiss on the mouth before we all went inside.

The place was small and muddy and smelled like stale rain and had a large unmade bed that looked as if it had been a partner to some of the saddest love-making this side of The Cross.

There was a green bushy half-table with a couple of insect-like chairs and a little sink and a small stove that was used for cooking and heating.

There were some dirty dishes in the little sink. The dishes looked as if they had always been dirty: born dirty to last forever.

I could hear a radio playing Western music someplace in the trailer, but I couldn't find it. I looked all over but it was nowhere in sight. It was probably under a shirt or something.

"He's the kid with the typewriter," she said. "He'll get 1/3 for typing it."

"That sounds fair," he said. "We need somebody to type it. I've never done anything like this before."

"Why don't you show it to him?" she said. "He'd like to take a look at it."

"OK. But it isn't too carefully written," he said to me. "I only went to the fourth grade, so she's going to edit it, straighten out the grammar and commas and stuff."

There was a notebook lying on the table, next to an ash-tray that probably had 600 cigarette butts in it. The notebook had a color photograph of Hopalong Cassidy on the cover.

Hopalong looked tired as if he had spent the previous night chasing starlets all over Hollywood and barely had enough strength to get back in the saddle.

There were about twenty-five or thirty pages of writing in the notebook. It was written in a large grammar school sprawl: an unhappy marriage between printing and longhand.

"It's not finished yet," he said.

"You'll type it. I'll edit it. He'll write it," she said.

It was a story about a young logger falling in love with a waitress. The novel began in 1935 in a cafe in North Bend, Oregon.

The young logger was sitting at a table and the waitress was taking his order. She was very pretty with blond hair and rosy cheeks. The young logger was ordering veal cutlets with mashed potatoes and country gravy.

"Yeah, I'll do the editing. You can type it, can't you? It's not too bad, is it?" she said in a twelve-year-old voice with the Welfare peeking over her shoulder.

"No," I said. "It will be easy."

Suddenly the rain started to come down hard outside, without any warning, just suddenly great drops of rain that almost shook the trailer.

You sur lik veel cutlets dont you Maybell said she was ~~holdin~~ holding her pensil up her mowth that was preti and red like an apl!

Onli wen you tak my oder Carl said he was a kind of bassful loger but big and strong lik his dead who ownd the starmill!

Ill mak sur you get plenti of gravi!

Just ten the caf door opend and in cam Rins Adams he was hansom and meen, everi bodi in thos parts was afrad of him but not Carl and his ~~dead~~ dad they wasnt afrad of him no sur!

Maybell shifard wen she saw him standing ther in his blac macinaw he smild at her and Carl felt his blod run hot lik scallding cofee and fiting mad!

Howdi ther Rins said Maybell blushed like a ~~flower~~ flouar while we were all sitting there in that rainy trailer, pounding at the gates of American literature.

THE GATHERING
OF A CALIFORNIAN

LIKE most Californians, I come from someplace else and was gathered to the purpose of California like a metal-eating flower gathers the sunshine, the rain, and then to the freeway beckons its petals and lets the cars drive in, millions of cars into but a single flower, the scent choked with congestion and room for millions more.

California needs us, so it gathers us from other places. I'll take you, you, you, and I from the Pacific Northwest: a haunted land where nature dances the minuet with people and danced with me in those old bygone days.

I brought everything I knew from there to California: years and years of a different life to which I can never return nor want to and seems at times almost to have occurred to another body somehow vaguely in my shape and recognition.

It's strange that California likes to get her people from every place else and leave what we knew behind and here to California we are gathered as if energy itself, the shadow of that metal-eating flower, had summoned us away from other lives and now to do the California until the very end like the Taj Mahal in the shape of a parking meter.

A SHORT STORY ABOUT
CONTEMPORARY LIFE
IN CALIFORNIA

THERE are thousands of stories with original beginnings. This
is not one of them. I think the only way to start a story about
contemporary life in California is to do it the way Jack
London started *The Sea-Wolf*. I have confidence in that
beginning.

It worked in 1904 and it can work in 1969. I believe that
beginning can reach across the decades and serve the purpose
of this story because this is California—we can do anything
we want to do—and a rich young literary critic is taking a
ferryboat from Sausalito to San Francisco. He has just finished
spending a few days at a friend's cabin in Mill Valley. The
friend uses the cabin to read Schopenhauer and Nietzsche
during the winter. They all have great times together.

While travelling across the bay in the fog he thinks about
writing an essay called "The Necessity for Freedom: A Plea
for the Artist."

Of course Wolf Larsen torpedoes the ferryboat and cap-
tures the rich young literary critic who is changed instantly

into a cabin boy and has to wear funny clothes and take a lot of shit off everybody, has great intellectual conversations with old Wolf, gets kicked in the ass, grabbed by the throat, promoted to mate, grows up, meets his true love Maud, escapes from Wolf, bounces around the damn Pacific Ocean in little better than a half-assed rowboat, finds an island, builds a stone hut, clubs seals, fixes a broken sailing ship, buries Wolf at sea, gets kissed, etc.: all to end this story about contemporary life in California sixty-five years later.

Thank God.

PACIFIC RADIO FIRE

THE largest ocean in the world starts or ends at Monterey, California. It depends on what language you are speaking. My friend's wife had just left him. She walked right out the door and didn't even say good-bye. We went and got two fifths of port and headed for the Pacific.

It's an old song that's been played on all the jukeboxes in America. The song has been around so long that it's been recorded on the very dust of America and it has settled on everything and changed chairs and cars and toys and lamps and windows into billions of phonographs to play that song back into the ear of our broken heart.

We sat down on a small corner-like beach surrounded by big granite rocks and the hugeness of the Pacific Ocean with all its vocabularies.

We were listening to rock and roll on his transistor radio and somberly drinking port. We were both in despair. I didn't know what he was going to do with the rest of his life either.

I took another sip of port. The Beach Boys were singing a song about California girls on the radio. They liked them.

His eyes were wet wounded rugs.

Like some kind of strange vacuum cleaner I tried to console him. I recited the same old litanies that you say to people when you try to help their broken hearts, but words can't help at all.

It's just the sound of another human voice that makes the only difference. There's nothing you're ever going to say that's going to make anybody happy when they're feeling shitty about losing somebody that they love.

Finally he set fire to the radio. He piled some paper around it. He struck a match to the paper. We sat there watching it. I had never seen anybody set fire to a radio before.

As the radio gently burned away, the flames began to affect the songs that we were listening to. A record that was #1 on the Top-40 suddenly dropped to #13 inside of itself. A song that was #9 became #27 in the middle of a chorus about loving somebody. They tumbled in popularity like broken birds. Then it was too late for all of them.

ELMIRA

I return as if in the dream of a young American duck hunting prince to Elmira and I am standing again on the bridge across the Long Tom River. It is always late December and the river is high and muddy and stirs dark leafless branches from its cold depths.

Sometimes it is raining on the bridge and I'm looking downstream to where the river flows into the lake. There is always a marshy field in my dream surrounded by an old black wooden fence and an ancient shed showing light through the walls and the roof.

I'm warm and dry under sweet layers of royal underwear and rain clothes.

Sometimes it is cold and clear and I can see my breath and there's frost on the bridge and I'm looking upstream into a tangle of trees that lead to the mountains many miles away where the Long Tom River starts its beginning.

Sometimes I write my name on the bridge in frost. I spell

my name out very carefully, and sometimes I write "Elmira" in frost, too, and just as carefully.

I'm always carrying a double-barrel sixteen-gauge shotgun with lots of shells in my pockets . . . perhaps too many shells because I am a teen-ager and it's easy to worry about running out of shells, so I'm weighed down with too many shells.

I'm almost like a deep-sea diver because my pockets are filled with such an abundance of lead. Sometimes I even walk funny because I've got so many shells in my pockets.

I'm always alone on the bridge and there's always a small flock of mallards that fly very high over the bridge and down toward the lake.

Sometimes I look both ways on the road to see if a car is coming and if a car isn't coming, I shoot at them, but they are too high for my shot to do anything but annoy them a little.

Sometimes a car is coming and I just watch the ducks fly down the river and keep the shooting to myself. It might be a game warden or a deputy sheriff. I have an idea somewhere in my head that it is against the law to shoot at ducks from a bridge. .

I wonder if I am right.

Sometimes I don't look to see if there is a car on the road. The ducks are too high to shoot at. I know I'll just waste my ammunition, so I let them pass.

The ducks are always a flock of fat mallards just in from Canada.

Sometimes I walk through the little town of Elmira and everything is very quiet because it's so early in the morning and God forsaken with either rain or cold.

Whenever I walk through Elmira, I stand and look at the

Elmira Union High School. The classrooms are always empty
and dark inside. It seems as if nobody ever studies there and
the darkness is never broken because there is no reason to
ever turn the lights on.

Sometimes I don't go into Elmira. I cross over the black
wooden fence and go into the marshy field and walk past the
ancient religious shed and follow the river down to the lake,
hoping to hit some good duck hunting.

I never do.

Elmira is very beautiful but it is not a lucky place for me
to hunt.

I always get to Elmira by hitch-hiking about twenty miles.
I stand out there in the cold or the rain with my shotgun,
wearing my royal duck hunting robes and people stop and
pick me up, and that's how I get there.

"Where are you going?" people say when I get in. I sit
beside them with my shotgun balanced like a scepter between
my legs and the barrels pointing up at the roof. The gun is at
an angle, so the barrels point toward the passenger side of the
roof, and I'm always the passenger.

"Elmira."

COFFEE

SOMETIMES life is merely a matter of coffee and whatever intimacy a cup of coffee affords. I once read something about coffee. The thing said that coffee is good for you; it stimulates all the organs.

I thought at first this was a strange way to put it, and not altogether pleasant, but as time goes by I have found out that it makes sense in its own limited way. I'll tell you what I mean.

Yesterday morning I went over to see a girl. I like her. Whatever we had going for us is gone now. She does not care for me. I blew it and wish I hadn't.

I rang the door bell and waited on the stairs. I could hear her moving around upstairs. The way she moved I could tell that she was getting up. I had awakened her.

Then she came down the stairs. I could feel her approach in my stomach. Every step she took stirred my feelings and led indirectly to her opening the door. She saw me and it did not please her.

Once upon a time it pleased her very much, last week. I wonder where it went, pretending to be naive.

"I feel strange now," she said. "I don't want to talk."

"I want a cup of coffee," I said, because it was the last thing in the world that I wanted. I said it in such a way that it sounded as if I were reading her a telegram from somebody else, a person who really wanted a cup of coffee, who cared about nothing else.

"All right," she said.

I followed her up the stairs. It was ridiculous. She had just put some clothes on. They had not quite adjusted themselves to her body. I could tell you about her ass. We went into the kitchen.

She took a jar of instant coffee off a shelf and put it on the table. She placed a cup next to it, and a spoon. I looked at them. She put a pan full of water on the stove and turned the gas on under it.

All this time she did not say a word. Her clothes adjusted themselves to her body. I won't. She left the kitchen.

Then she went down the stairs and outside to see if she had any mail. I didn't remember seeing any. She came back up the stairs and went into another room. She closed the door after her. I looked at the pan full of water on the stove.

I knew that it would take a year before the water started to boil. It was now October and there was too much water in the pan. That was the problem. I threw half the water into the sink.

The water would boil faster now. It would take only six months. The house was quiet.

I looked out at the back porch. There were sacks of garbage there. I stared at the garbage and tried to figure out what she had been eating lately by studying the containers and peelings and stuff. I couldn't tell a thing.

It was now March. The water started to boil. I was pleased by this.

I looked at the table. There was the jar of instant coffee, the empty cup and the spoon all laid out like a funeral service. These are the things that you need to make a cup of coffee.

When I left the house ten minutes later, the cup of coffee safely inside me like a grave, I said, "Thank you for the cup of coffee."

"You're welcome," she said. Her voice came from behind a closed door. Her voice sounded like another telegram. It was really time for me to leave.

I spent the rest of the day not making coffee. It was a comfort. And evening came. I had dinner in a restaurant and went to a bar. I had some drinks and talked to some people.

We were bar people and said bar things. None of them remembered, and the bar closed. It was two o'clock in the morning. I had to go outside. It was foggy and cold in San Francisco. I wondered about the fog and felt very human and exposed.

I decided to go visit another girl. We had not been friends for over a year. Once we were very close. I wondered what she was thinking about now.

I went over to her house. She didn't have a door bell. That was a small victory. One must keep track of all the small victories. I do, anyway.

She answered the door. She was holding a robe in front of herself. She didn't believe that she was seeing me. "What do you want?" she said, believing now that she was seeing me. I walked right into the house.

She turned and closed the door in such a way that I could see her profile. She had not bothered to wrap the robe completely around herself. She was just holding the robe in front of herself.

I could see an unbroken line of body running from her head to her feet. It looked kind of strange. Perhaps because it was so late at night.

"What do you want?" she said.

"I want a cup of coffee," I said. What a funny thing to say, to say again for a cup of coffee was not what I really wanted.

She looked at me and wheeled slightly on the profile. She was not pleased to see me. Let the AMA tell us that time heals. I looked at the unbroken line of her body.

"Why don't you have a cup of coffee with me?" I said. "I feel like talking to you. We haven't talked for a long time."

She looked at me and wheeled slightly on the profile. I stared at the unbroken line of her body. This was not good.

"It's too late," she said. "I have to get up in the morning. If you want a cup of coffee, there's instant in the kitchen. I have to go to bed."

The kitchen light was on. I looked down the hall into the kitchen. I didn't feel like going into the kitchen and having another cup of coffee by myself. I didn't feel like going to anybody else's house and asking them for a cup of coffee.

I realized that the day had been committed to a very strange pilgrimage, and I had not planned it that way. At least the jar of instant coffee was not on the table, beside an empty white cup and a spoon.

They say in the spring a young man's fancy turns to thoughts of love. Perhaps if he has enough time left over, his fancy can even make room for a cup of coffee.

THE LOST CHAPTERS OF
TROUT FISHING IN AMERICA:
"REMBRANDT CREEK"
AND "CARTHAGE SINK"

THESE two chapters were lost in the late winter, early spring of 1961. I looked all over for them but I couldn't find them anywhere. I haven't the slightest idea why I didn't rewrite them as soon as I realized that they were gone. It's a real puzzler but I didn't and now eight years later, I've decided to return to the winter that I was twenty-six years old, living on Greenwich Street in San Francisco, married, had an infant daughter and wrote these two chapters toward a vision of America and then lost them. I'm going back there now to see if I can find them.

"REMBRANDT CREEK"

REMBRANDT Creek looked just like its name and it was in lonely country that had very bad winters. The creek started in a high mountain meadow surrounded by pine trees. That

was about the only real light that creek ever saw because
after it had gathered itself from some small springs in the
meadow, it flowed off into the pines and down to a dark-tree-
tangled canyon that went along the edge of the mountains.

The creek was filled with little trout so wild that they were
barely afraid when you walked up to the creek and stood
there staring down at them.

I never really went fishing for them in any classical or even
functioning sense. The only reason I knew that creek was
because that's where we camped when we went deer hunting.

No, it was not a fishing creek for me but just a place where
we got water that we needed for our camp but I seemed to
carry most of the water that we used and I think I washed a
lot of dishes because I was the teen-ager and it was easier to
have me do those things than the men who were older and
wiser and needed time to think about places where deer might
be and also to drink a little whiskey which seemed to aid
thoughts of hunting and other things.

"Hey, kid, take your head out of your ass and see if you
can do something about these dishes." That was one of the
elders of the hunt speaking. His voice is remembered down
trails of sound-colored hunting marble.

Often I think about Rembrandt Creek and how much it
looked like a painting hanging in the world's largest museum
with a roof that went to the stars and galleries that knew the
whisk of comets.

I only fished it once.

I didn't have any fishing tackle, just a 30:30 Winchester,
so I took an old rusty bent nail and tied some white string
onto it like the ghost of my childhood and tried to catch a
trout using a piece of deer meat for bait and I almost caught
one, too, lifting it out of the water just before it fell off my
nail and back into the painting that carried it from my sight,

returning it to the Seventeenth Century where it belonged on the easel of a man named Rembrandt.

"CARTHAGE SINK"

THE Carthage River came roaring out of the ground at a fountainhead that was like a wild well. It flowed arrogantly a dozen miles or so through an open canyon and then just disappeared into the ground at a place that was called Carthage Sink.

The river loved to tell everybody (everybody being the sky, the wind, the few trees that grew around there, birds, deer and even the stars if you can believe that) what a great river it was.

"I come roaring from the earth and return roaring to the earth. I am the master of my waters. I am the mother and father of myself. I don't need a single drop of rain. Look at my smooth strong white muscles. I am my own future!"

The Carthage River kept this kind of talking up for thousands of years. Needless to say: Everybody (everybody being the sky, etc.) was bored up to here with that river.

Birds and deer tried to keep away from that part of the country if they could avoid it. The stars had been reduced to playing a waiting game and there was a dramatically noticeable lack of wind in that area, except of course for the Carthage River.

Even the trout that lived there were ashamed of the river and always glad when they died. Anything was better than living in that God-damn bombastic river.

One day the Carthage River in mid-breath telling about how great it was, dried up, "I am the master of my . . ." It just stopped.

The river couldn't believe it. Not one more drop of water came from the ground and its sink was soon just a trickle dripping back into the ground like the runny nose of a kid.

The Carthage River's pride vanished in an irony of water and the canyon turned into a good mood. Birds suddenly flew all over the place and took a happy look at what had happened and a great wind came up and it even seemed as if the stars were out earlier that night to take a look and then smile beatifically.

There was a summer rainstorm a few miles away in some mountains and the Carthage River begged for the rain to come to its rescue.

"Please," the river said with a voice that was now only the shadow of a whisper. "Help me. I need water for my trout. They're dying. Look at the poor little things."

The storm looked at the trout. The trout were very happy with the way things were now, though they would soon be dead.

The rainstorm made up some incredibly elaborate story about having to visit somebody's grandmother who had a broken ice-cream freezer and somehow lots of rain was needed to repair it, "But maybe in a few months we might get together. I'll call you on the telephone before I come over."

The next day which was of course August 17, 1921 a lot of people, townspeople and such, drove out in their cars and looked at the former river and shook their heads in wonder. They had a lot of picnic baskets with them, too.

There was an article in the local paper with two photographs showing two large empty holes that had been the fountainhead and the sink of the Carthage River. The holes looked like nostrils.

Another photograph was of a cowboy sitting on his horse,

holding an umbrella in one hand and pointing into the depths of the Carthage Sink with his other hand. He was looking very serious. It was a photograph to make people laugh and that's exactly what they did.

Well, there you have the lost chapters of *Trout Fishing in America*. Their style is probably a little different because I'm a little different now, I'm thirty-four, and they were probably written in a slightly different form, too. It's interesting that I didn't rewrite them back there in 1961 but waited until December 4, 1969, almost a decade later, to return and try to bring them back with me.

THE WEATHER IN
SAN FRANCISCO

IT was a cloudy afternoon with an Italian butcher selling a pound of meat to a very old woman, but who knows what such an old woman could possibly use a pound of meat for?

She was too old for that much meat. Perhaps she used it for a bee hive and she had five hundred golden bees at home waiting for the meat, their bodies stuffed with honey.

"What kind of meat would you like today?" the butcher said. "We have some good hamburger. It's lean."

"I don't know," she said. "Hamburger is something else."

"Yeah, it's lean. I ground it myself. I put a lot of lean meat in it."

"Hamburger doesn't sound right," she said.

"Yeah," the butcher said. "It's a good day for hamburger. Look outside. It's cloudy. Some of those clouds have rain in them. I'd get the hamburger," he said.

"No," she said. "I don't want any hamburger, and I don't think it's going to rain. I think the sun is going to come out, and it will be a beautiful day, and I want a pound of liver."

The butcher was stunned. He did not like to sell liver to old ladies. There was something about it that made him very nervous. He didn't want to talk to her any more.

He reluctantly sliced a pound of liver off a huge red chunk and wrapped it up in white paper and put it into a brown bag. It was a very unpleasant experience for him.

He took her money, gave her the change, and went back to the poultry section to try and get a hold of his nerves.

By using her bones like the sails of a ship, the old woman passed outside into the street. She carried the liver as if it were a victory to the bottom of a very steep hill.

She climbed the hill and being very old, it was hard on her. She grew tired and had to stop and rest many times before she reached the top.

At the top of the hill was the old woman's house: a tall San Francisco house with bay windows that reflected a cloudy day.

She opened her purse which was like a small autumn field and near the fallen branches of an old apple tree, she found her keys.

Then she opened the door. It was a dear and trusted friend. She nodded at the door and went into the house and walked down a long hall into a room that was filled with bees.

There were bees everywhere in the room. Bees on the chairs. Bees on the photograph of her dead parents. Bees on the curtains. Bees on an ancient radio that once listened to the 1930s. Bees on her comb and brush.

The bees came to her and gathered about her lovingly while she unwrapped the liver and placed it upon a cloudy silver platter that soon changed into a sunny day.

COMPLICATED BANKING
PROBLEMS

I have a bank account because I grew tired of burying my money in the back yard and something else happened. I was burying some money a few years ago when I came across a human skeleton.

The skeleton had the remains of a shovel in one hand and a half-dissolved coffee can in the other hand. The coffee can was filled with a kind of rustdust material that I think was once money, so now I have a bank account.

But most of the time that doesn't work out very well either. When I wait in line there are almost always people in front of me who have complicated banking problems. I have to stand there and endure the financial cartoon crucifixions of America.

It goes something like this: There are three people in front of me. I have a little check to cash. My banking will only take a minute. The check is already endorsed. I have it in my hand, pointed in the direction of the teller.

The person just being waited on now is a woman fifty years

old. She is wearing a long black coat, though it is a hot day. She appears to be very comfortable in the coat and there is a strange smell coming from her. I think about it for a few seconds and realize that this is the first sign of a complicated banking problem.

Then she reaches into the folds of her coat and removes the shadow of a refrigerator filled with sour milk and year-old carrots. She wants to put the shadow in her savings account. She's already made out the slip.

I look up at the ceiling of the bank and pretend that it is the Sistine Chapel.

The old woman puts up quite a struggle before she's taken away. There's a lot of blood on the floor. She bit an ear off one of the guards.

I guess you have to admire her spunk.

The check in my hand is for ten dollars.

The next two people in line are actually one person. They are a pair of Siamese twins, but they each have their own bank books.

One of them is putting eighty-two dollars in his savings account and the other one is closing his savings account. The teller counts out 3,574 dollars for him and he puts it away in the pocket on his side of the pants.

All of this takes time. I look up at the ceiling of the bank again but I cannot pretend that it is the Sistine Chapel any more. My check is sweaty as if it had been written in 1929.

The last person between me and the teller is totally anonymous looking. He is so anonymous that he's barely there.

He puts 237 checks down on the counter that he wants to deposit in his checking account. They are for a total of 489,000 dollars. He also has 611 checks that he wants to deposit in his savings account. They are for a total of 1,754,961 dollars.

His checks completely cover the counter like a success snow storm. The teller starts on his banking as if she were a long distance runner while I stand there thinking that the skeleton in the back yard had made the right decision after all.

A HIGH BUILDING
IN SINGAPORE

IT's a high building in Singapore that holds the only beauty for this San Francisco day where I am walking down the street, feeling terrible and watching my mind function with the efficiency of a liquid pencil.

A young mother passes by talking to her little girl who is really too small to be able to talk, but she's talking anyway and very excitedly to her mother about something. I can't quite make out what she is saying because she's so little.

I mean, this is a tiny kid.

Then her mother answers her to explode my day with a goofy illumination. "It was a high building in Singapore," she says to the little girl who enthusiastically replies like a bright sound-colored penny, "Yes, it was a high building in Singapore!"

AN UNLIMITED SUPPLY
OF 35 MILLIMETER FILM

PEOPLE cannot figure out why he is with her. They don't understand. He's so good-looking and she's so plain. "What does he see in her?" they ask themselves and each other. They know it's not her cooking because she's not a good cook. About the only thing that she can cook is a halfway decent meat loaf. She makes it every Tuesday night and he has a meat loaf sandwich in his lunch on Wednesday. Years pass. They stay together while their friends break up.

The beginning answer, as in so many of these things, lies in the bed where they make love. She becomes the theater where he shows films of his sexual dreams. Her body is like soft rows of living theater seats leading to a vagina that is the warm screen of his imagination where he makes love to all the women that he sees and wants like passing quicksilver movies, but she doesn't know a thing about it.

All she knows is that she loves him very much and he always pleases her and makes her feel good. She gets excited around four o'clock in the afternoon because she knows that he will be home from work at five.

He has made love to hundreds of different women inside of her. She makes all his dreams come true as she lies there like a simple contented theater in his touching, thinking only of him.

"What does he see in her?" people go on asking themselves and each other. They should know better. The final answer is very simple. It's all in his head.

THE SCARLATTI TILT

"IT's very hard to live in a studio apartment in San Jose with a man who's learning to play the violin." That's what she told the police when she handed them the empty revolver.

THE WILD BIRDS
OF HEAVEN

I'd rather dwell in some dark holler
where the sun refuses to shine,
where the wild birds of heaven
can't hear me when I whine.

—Folk Song

THAT'S right. The children had been complaining for weeks about the television set. The picture was going out and that death John Donne spoke so fondly about was advancing rapidly down over the edge of whatever was playing that night, and there were also static lines that danced now and then like drunken cemeteries on that picture.

Mr. Henly was a simple American man, but his children were reaching the end of their rope. He worked in an insurance office keeping the dead separated from the living. They were in filing cabinets. Everybody at the office said that he had a great future.

One day he came home from work and his children were

waiting for him. They laid it right on the line: either he bought a new television set or they would become juvenile delinquents.

They showed him a photograph of five juvenile delinquents raping an old woman. One of the juvenile delinquents was hitting her on the head with a bicycle chain.

Mr. Henly agreed instantly to the children's demands. Anything, just put away that awful photograph. Then his wife came in and said the kindest thing she had said to him since the children were born, "Get a new television set for the kids. What are you: some kind of human monster?"

The next day Mr. Henly found himself standing in front of the Frederick Crow Department Store, and there was a huge sign plastered over the window. The sign said poetically: TV SALE.

He went inside and immediately found a video pacifier that had a 42-inch screen with built-in umbilical ducts. A clerk came over and sold the set to him by saying, "Hi, there."

"I'll take it," Mr. Henly said.

"Cash or credit?"

"Credit."

"Do you have one of our credit cards?" The clerk looked down at Mr. Henly's feet. "No, you don't have one," he said. "Just give me your name and address and the television set will be home when you get there."

"What about my credit?" Mr. Henly said.

"That won't be any problem," the clerk said. "Our credit department is waiting for you."

"Oh," Mr. Henly said.

The clerk pointed the way back to the credit department. "They're waiting for you."

The clerk was right, too. There was a beautiful girl sitting at a desk. She was really lovely. She looked like a composite of all the beautiful girls you see in all the cigarette advertisements and on television.

Wow! Mr. Henly took out his pack and lit up. After all he was no fool.

The girl smiled and said, "May I help you?"

"Yes. I want to buy a television set on credit, and I'd like to open an account at your store. I have a steady job, three children and I'm buying a house and a car. My credit's good," he said. "I'm already 25,000 dollars in debt."

Mr. Henly expected the girl to make a telephone call to check on his credit or do something to see if he had been lying about the 25,000 dollars.

She didn't.

"Don't worry about anything," she said. She certainly did have a nice voice. "The set is yours. Just step in there."

She pointed toward a room that had a pleasant door. Actually the door was quite exciting. It was a heavy wooden door with a fantastic grain running through the wood, a grain like the cracks of an earthquake running across the desert sunrise. The grain was filled with light.

The doorknob was pure silver. It was the door that Mr. Henly had always wanted to open. His hand had dreamt its shape while millions of years had passed in the sea.

Above the door was a sign:

BLACKSMITH.

He opened the door and went inside and there was a man waiting for him. The man said, "Take off your shoes, please."

"I just want to sign the papers," Mr. Henly said. "I've got a steady job. I'll pay on time."

"Don't worry about it," the man said. "Just take off your shoes."

Mr. Henly took off his shoes.

"The socks, too."

He did this and then did not think it strange because after all he didn't have any money to buy the television set with. The floor wasn't cold.

"How tall are you?" the man asked.

"5-11."

The man walked over to a filing cabinet and pulled out the drawer that had 5-11 printed on it. The man took out a plastic bag and then closed the drawer. Mr. Henly thought of a good joke to tell the man but then immediately forgot it.

The man opened the bag and took out the shadow of an immense bird. He unfolded the shadow as if it were a pair of pants.

"What's that?"

"It's the shadow of a bird," the man said and walked over to where Mr. Henly was sitting and laid the shadow on the floor beside his feet.

Then he took a strange-looking hammer and pulled the nails out of Mr. Henly's shadow, the nails that fastened it to his body. The man folded up the shadow very carefully. He laid it on a chair beside Mr. Henly.

"What are you doing?" Mr. Henly said. He wasn't afraid. Just a little curious.

"Putting the shadow on," the man said and nailed the bird's shadow onto his feet. At least it didn't hurt.

"There you go," the man said. "You have 24 months to pay for the television set. When you finish paying for the set, we'll switch shadows. It looks pretty good on you."

Mr. Henly stared down at the shadow of a bird coming off his human body. It doesn't look bad, Mr. Henly thought.

When he left the room the beautiful girl behind the desk said, "My, how you've changed."

Mr. Henly liked having her talk to him. During many years of married life he had forgotten what sex was really about.

He reached into his pocket for a cigarette and discovered that he had smoked them all up. He felt very embarrassed. The girl stared at him as if he were a small child that had done something wrong.

WINTER RUG

MY credentials? Of course. They are in my pocket. Here: I've had friends who have died in California and I mourn them in my own way. I've been to Forest Lawn and romped over the place like an eager child. I've read *The Loved One, The American Way of Death, Wallets in Shrouds* and my favorite *After Many a Summer Dies the Swan.*

I have watched men standing beside hearses in front of mortuaries directing funerals with walky-talkies as if they were officers in a metaphysical war.

Oh, yes: I was once walking with a friend past a skid row hotel in San Francisco and they were carrying a corpse out of the hotel. The corpse was done tastefully in a white sheet with four or five Chinese extras looking on, and there was a very slow-moving ambulance parked out front that was prohibited by law from having a siren or to go any faster than thirty-seven miles an hour and from showing any aggressive action in traffic.

My friend looked at the lady or gentleman corpse as it went by and said, "Being dead is one step up from living in that hotel."

As you can see, I am an expert on death in California. My credentials stand up to the closest inspection. I am qualified to continue with another story told to me by my friend who also works as a gardener for a very wealthy old woman in Marin County. She had a nineteen-year-old dog that she loved deeply and the dog responded to this love by dying very slowly from senility.

Every day my friend went to work the dog would be a little more dead. It was long past the proper time for the dog to die, but the dog had been dying for so long that it had lost the way to death.

This happens to a lot of old people in this country. They get so old and live with death so long that they lose the way when it comes time to actually die.

Sometimes they stay lost for years. It is horrible to watch them linger on. Finally the weight of their own blood crushes them.

Anyway, at last the woman could not stand to watch the senile suffering of her dog any longer and called up a veterinarian to come and put the dog to sleep.

She instructed my friend to build a coffin for the dog, which he did, figuring it was one of the fringe clauses of gardening in California.

The death doctor drove out to her estate and was soon in the house carrying a little black bag. That was a mistake. It should have been a large pastel bag. When the old woman saw the little black bag, she paled visibly. The unnecessary reality of it scared her, so she sent the veterinarian away with a generous check in his pocket.

Alas, having the veterinarian go away did not solve the dog's basic problem: He was so senile that death had become a way of life and he was lost from the act of dying.

The next day the dog walked into the corner of a room and couldn't get out of it. The dog stood there for hours until it collapsed from exhaustion, which conveniently happened to be just when the old woman came into the room, looking for the keys to her Rolls-Royce.

She started crying when she saw the dog lying there like a mutt puddle in the corner. Its face was still pressed against the wall and its eyes were watering in some human kind of way that dogs get when they live with people too long and pick up their worst characteristics.

She had her maid carry the dog to his rug. The dog had a Chinese rug that he had slept on since he was a puppy in China before the fall of Chiang Kai-shek. The rug had been worth a thousand American dollars, then, having survived a dynasty or two.

The rug was worth a lot more now, being in rather excellent shape with actually no more wear and tear than it would get being stored in a castle for a couple of centuries.

The old woman called the veterinarian again and he arrived with his little black bag of tricks and how to find the way back to death after having lost it for years, years that led oneself to being trapped in the corner of a room.

"Where is your pet?" he said.

"On his rug," she said.

The dog lay exhausted and sprawled across beautiful Chinese flowers and things from a different world. "Please do it on his rug," she said. "I think he would like that."

"Certainly," he said. "Don't worry. He won't feel a thing. It's painless. Just like falling asleep."

"Good-bye, Charlie," the old woman said. The dog of course didn't hear her. He had been deaf since 1959.

After bidding the dog farewell, the old woman took to bed. She left the room just as the veterinarian was opening his little black bag. The veterinarian needed PR help desperately.

Afterward my friend took the coffin in the house to pick up the dog. A maid had wrapped the body in the rug. The old woman insisted that the dog be buried with the rug and its head facing West in a grave near the rose garden, pointing toward China. My friend buried the dog with its head pointing toward Los Angeles.

As he carried the coffin outside he peeked in at the thousand-dollar rug. Beautiful design, he said to himself. All you would have to do would be to vacuum it a little and it would be as good as new.

My friend is not generally known as a sentimentalist. Stupid dead dog! he said to himself as he neared the grave, Damn dead dog!

"But I did it," he told me. "I buried that dog with the rug and I don't know why. It's a question that I'll ask myself forever. Sometimes when it rains at night in the winter, I think of that rug down there in the grave, wrapped around a dog."

ERNEST HEMINGWAY'S
TYPIST

IT sounds like religious music. A friend of mine just came back from New York where he had Ernest Hemingway's typist do some typing for him.

He's a successful writer, so he went and got the very best, which happens to be the woman who did Ernest Hemingway's typing. It's enough to take your breath away, to marble your lungs with silence.

Ernest Hemingway's typist!

She's every young writer's dream come true with the appearance of her hands which are like a harpsichord and the perfect intensity of her gaze and all to be followed by the profound sound of her typing.

He paid her fifteen dollars an hour. That's more money than a plumber or an electrician gets.

$120 a day! for a typist!

He said that she does everything for you. You just hand her the copy and like a miracle you have attractive, correct spelling and punctuation that is so beautiful that it brings

tears to your eyes and paragraphs that look like Greek temples
and she even finishes sentences for you.

   She's Ernest Hemingway's
   She's Ernest Hemingway's typist.

HOMAGE
TO THE SAN FRANCISCO
YMCA

ONCE upon a time in San Francisco there was a man who really liked the finer things in life, especially poetry. He liked good verse.

He could afford to indulge himself in this liking, which meant that he didn't have to work because he was receiving a generous pension that was the result of a 1920s investment that his grandfather had made in a private insane asylum that was operating quite profitably in Southern California.

In the black, as they say and located in the San Fernando Valley, just outside of Tarzana. It was one of those places that do not look like an insane asylum. It looked like something else with flowers all around it, mostly roses.

The checks always arrived on the 1st and the 15th of every month, even when there was not a mail delivery on that day. He had a lovely house in Pacific Heights and he would go out and buy more poetry. He of course had never met a poet in person. That would have been a little too much.

One day he decided that his liking for poetry could not be

fully expressed in just reading poetry or listening to poets reading on phonograph records. He decided to take the plumbing out of his house and completely replace it with poetry, and so he did.

He turned off the water and took out the pipes and put in John Donne to replace them. The pipes did not look too happy. He took out his bathtub and put in William Shakespeare. The bathtub did not know what was happening.

He took out his kitchen sink and put in Emily Dickinson. The kitchen sink could only stare back in wonder. He took out his bathroom sink and put in Vladimir Mayakovsky. The bathroom sink, even though the water was off, broke out into tears.

He took out his hot water heater and put in Michael McClure's poetry. The hot water heater could barely contain its sanity. Finally he took out his toilet and put in the minor poets. The toilet planned on leaving the country.

And now the time had come to see how it all worked, to enjoy the fruit of his amazing labor. Christopher Columbus' slight venture sailing West was merely the shadow of a dismal event in the comparison. He turned the water back on again and surveyed the countenance of his vision brought to reality. He was a happy man.

"I think I'll take a bath," he said, to celebrate. He tried to heat up some Michael McClure to take a bath in some William Shakespeare and what happened was not actually what he had planned on happening.

"Might as well do the dishes, then," he said. He tried to wash some plates in "I taste a liquor never brewed," and found there was quite a difference between that liquid and a kitchen sink. Despair was on its way.

He tried to go to the toilet and the minor poets did not do at all. They began gossiping about their careers as he sat there trying to take a shit. One of them had written 197 sonnets about a penguin he had once seen in a travelling circus. He sensed a Pulitzer Prize in this material.

Suddenly the man realized that poetry could not replace plumbing. It's what they call seeing the light. He decided immediately to take the poetry out and put the pipes back in, along with the sinks, the bathtub, the hot water heater and the toilet.

"This just didn't work out the way I planned it," he said. "I'll have to put the plumbing back. Take the poetry out." It made sense standing there naked in the total light of failure.

But then he ran into more trouble than there was in the first place. The poetry did not want to go. It liked very much occupying the positions of the former plumbing.

"I look great as a kitchen sink," Emily Dickinson's poetry said.

"We look wonderful as a toilet," the minor poets said.

"I'm grand as pipes," John Donne's poetry said.

"I'm a perfect hot water heater," Michael McClure's poetry said.

Vladimir Mayakovsky sang new faucets from the bathroom, there are faucets beyond suffering, and William Shakespeare's poetry was nothing but smiles.

"That's well and dandy for you," the man said. "But I have to have plumbing, *real* plumbing in this house. Did you notice the emphasis I put on *real*? Real! Poetry just can't handle it. Face up to reality," the man said to the poetry.

But the poetry refused to go. "We're staying." The man offered to call the police. "Go ahead and lock us up, you illiterate," the poetry said in one voice.

"I'll call the fire department!"

"Book burner!" the poetry shouted.

The man began to fight the poetry. It was the first time

he had ever been in a fight. He kicked the poetry of Emily Dickinson in the nose.

Of course the poetry of Michael McClure and Vladimir Mayakovsky walked over and said in English and in Russian, "That won't do at all," and threw the man down a flight of stairs. He got the message.

That was two years ago. The man is now living in the YMCA in San Francisco and loves it. He spends more time in the bathroom than everybody else. He goes in there at night and talks to himself with the light out.

THE PRETTY OFFICE

WHEN first I passed by there, it was just an ordinary office with desks and typewriters and filing cabinets and telephones ringing and people answering the telephones. There were half a dozen women working there, but there was nothing to distinguish them from millions of other office workers across America, and none of them were pretty.

The men who worked in the office were all about middle age and they did not show any sign of ever having been handsome in their youth or actually anything in their youth. They all looked like people whose names you forget.

They did what they had to do in the office. There was no sign on the window or above the door telling what the office was about, so I never knew what those people were doing. Perhaps they were a division of a large business that was located someplace else.

The people all seemed to know what they were doing, and so I let it go at that, passing by there twice a day: on my way to work and on my way home from work.

A year or so passed and the office remained constant. The people were the same and a certain amount of activity went on: just another little place in the universe.

Then one day I passed by there on my way to work and all the ordinary women who had worked there were gone, vanished, as if the very air itself had given them new employment.

There was not even a trace of them, and in their wake were six very pretty girls: blondes and brunettes and on and on into the various pretty faces and bodies, into the exciting feminine of this and that, into form-fitting smart clothes.

There were large friendly-looking breasts and small pleasant breasts and behinds that were all enticing. Every place I looked in that office there was something nice happening in woman form.

What had happened? Where had the other women gone? Where had these women come from? They all looked new to San Francisco. Whose idea was this? Was this the ultimate meaning of Frankenstein? My God, we all guessed wrong!

And now it's been another year with passing by there five days a week and staring intently in the window, trying to figure it out: all these pretty bodies carrying on whatever they do in there.

I wonder if the boss's wife, whoever the boss is, which one he is, died and this is his revenge over years of dullness, getting even it's called, or maybe he just got tired of watching television in the evening.

Or just what happened, I don't know.

There is a girl with long blond hair answering the telephone. There is a cute brunette putting something away in a filing cabinet. There is a cheer leader type with perfect teeth erasing something. There is an exotic brunette carrying a book across the office. There is a mysterious little girl with very large breasts rolling a piece of paper into a typewriter. There is a tall girl with a perfect mouth and a grand behind, putting a stamp on an envelope.

It's a pretty office.

A NEED FOR GARDENS

WHEN I got there they were burying the lion in the back yard again. As usual, it was a hastily dug grave, not really large enough to hold the lion and dug with a maximum of incompetence and they were trying to stuff the lion into a sloppy little hole.

The lion as usual took it quite stoically. Having been buried at least fifty times during the last two years, the lion had gotten used to being buried in the back yard.

I remember the first time they buried him. He didn't know what was happening. He was a younger lion, then, and was frightened and confused, but now he knew what was happening because he was an older lion and had been buried so many times.

He looked vaguely bored as they folded his front paws across his chest and started throwing dirt in his face.

It was basically hopeless. The lion would never fit the hole. It had never fit a hole in the back yard before and it never would. They just couldn't dig a hole big enough to bury that lion in.

"Hello," I said. "The hole's too small."

"Hello," they said. "No, it isn't."

This had been our standard greeting now for two years.

I stood there and watched them for an hour or so struggling desperately to bury the lion, but they were only able to bury ¼ of him before they gave up in disgust and stood around trying to blame each other for not making the hole big enough.

"Why don't you put a garden in next year?" I said. "This soil looks like it might grow some good carrots."

They didn't think that was very funny.

THE OLD BUS

I do what everybody else does: I live in San Francisco. Sometimes I am forced by Mother Nature to take the bus. Yesterday was an example. I wanted to get some place beyond the duty of my legs, far out on Clay Street, so I waited for a bus.

It was not a hardship but a nice warm autumn day and fiercely clear. An old woman waited, too. Nothing unusual about that, as they say. She had a large purse and white gloves that fit her hands like the skins of vegetables.

A Chinese fellow came by on the back of a motorcycle. It startled me. I had just never thought about the Chinese riding motorcycles before. Sometimes reality is an awfully close fit like the vegetable skins on that old woman's hands.

I was glad when the bus came. There is a certain happiness sighted when your bus comes along. It is of course a small specialized form of happiness and will never be a great thing.

I let the old woman get on first and trailed behind in classic medieval tradition with castle floors following me onto the bus.

I dropped in my fifteen cents, got my usual transfer, even though I did not need one. I always get a transfer. It gives me something to do with my hands while I am riding the bus. I *need* activity.

I sat down and looked the bus over to see who was there, and it took me about a minute to realize that there was something very wrong with that bus, and it took the other people about the same period to realize that there was something very wrong with the bus, and the thing that was wrong was me.

I was young. Everybody else on the bus, about nineteen of them, were men and women in their sixties, seventies and eighties, and I only in my twenties. They stared at me and I stared at them. We were all embarrassed and uncomfortable.

How had this happened? Why were we suddenly the players in this cruel fate and could not take our eyes off one another?

A man about seventy-eight began to clutch desperately at the lapel of his coat. A woman maybe sixty-three began to filter her hands, finger by finger, through a white handkerchief.

I felt terrible to remind them of their lost youth, their passage through slender years in such a cruel and unusual manner. Why were we tossed this way together as if we were nothing but a weird salad served on the seats of a God-damn bus?

I got off the bus at the next possibility. Everybody was glad to see me go and none of them were more glad than I.

I stood there and watched after the bus, its strange cargo now secure, growing distant in the journey of time until the bus was gone from sight.

THE GHOST CHILDREN
OF TACOMA

THE children of Tacoma, Washington, went to war in December 1941. It seemed like the thing to do, following in the footsteps of their parents and other grown-ups who acted as if they knew what was happening.

"Remember Pearl Harbor!" they said.

"You bet!" we said.

I was a child, then, though now I look like somebody else. We were at war in Tacoma. Children can kill imaginary enemies just as well as adults can kill real enemies. It went on for years.

During World War II, I personally killed 352,892 enemy soldiers without wounding one. Children need a lot less hospitals in war than grown-ups do. Children pretty much look at it from the alldeath side.

I sank 987 battleships, 532 aircraft carriers, 799 cruisers, 2,007 destroyers and 161 transport ships. Transports were not too interesting a target: very little sport.

I also sank 5,465 enemy PT boats. I have no idea why I

sank so many of them. It was just one of those things. Every time I turned around for four years, I was sinking a PT boat. I still wonder about that. 5,465 are a lot of PT boats.

I only sank three submarines. Submarines were just not up my alley. I sank my first submarine in the spring of 1942. A lot of kids rushed out and sank submarines right and left during December and January. I waited.

I waited until April, and then one morning on my way to school: BANG! my first sub., right in front of a grocery store. I sank my second submarine in 1944. I could afford to wait two years before sinking another one.

I sank my last submarine in February 1945, a few days after my tenth birthday. I was not totally satisfied with the presents I got that year.

And then there was the sky! I ventured forth into the sky, seeking the enemy there, while Mount Rainier towered up like a cold white general in the background.

I was an ace pilot with my P-38 and my Grumman Wildcat, my P-51 Mustang and my Messerschmitt. That's right: Messerschmitt. I captured one and had it painted a special color, so my own men wouldn't try to shoot me down by mistake. Everybody recognized my Messerschmitt and the enemy had hell to pay for it.

I shot down 8,942 fighter planes, 6,420 bombers and 51 blimps. I shot down most of the blimps when the war was first in season. Later, sometime in 1943, I stopped shooting down blimps altogether. Too slow.

I also destroyed 1,281 tanks, 777 bridges and 109 oil refineries because I knew we were in the right.

"Remember Pearl Harbor!" they said.

"You bet!" we said.

I shot the enemy planes down by holding out my arms

straight from my body and running like hell, shouting at the top of my lungs: RAT-tattattattattattattattattattattattat!

Children don't do that kind of stuff any more. Children do other things now and because children do other things now, I have whole days when I feel like the ghost of a child, examining the memory of toys played back into the earth again.

There was a thing I used to do that was also a lot of fun when I was a young airplane. I used to hunt up a couple of flashlights and hold them lit in my hands at night, with my arms straight out from my body and be a night pilot zooming down the streets of Tacoma.

I also used to play airplane in the house, too, by taking four chairs from the kitchen and putting them together: two chairs facing the same way for the fuselage and a chair for each wing.

In the house I played mostly at dive-bombing. The chairs seemed to do that best. My sister used to sit in the seat right behind me and radio urgent messages back to base.

"We only have one bomb left, but we can't let the aircraft carrier escape. We'll have to drop the bomb down the smoke-stack. Over. Thank you, Captain, we'll need all the luck we can get. Over and out."

Then my sister would say to me, "Do you think you can do it?" and I'd reply, "Of course, hang onto your hat."

Your Hat
Gone Now These
Twenty Years
January 1,
1965

TALK SHOW

I'M listening to a talk show on a new radio that I bought a few weeks ago. It's an AM/FM solid state white plastic radio. I very seldom buy anything new, so it was quite a surprise to my economy when I went into an Italian appliance store and bought this radio.

The salesman was very nice and told me that he had sold over four hundred of these radios to Italians who wanted to listen to an Italian language program that was on FM.

I don't know why but somehow that impressed me a great deal. It made me want to buy the radio, so that's how I surprised my economy.

The radio cost $29.95.

Now I'm listening to a talk show because it's raining hard outside and I've got nothing better to do with my ears. While I'm listening to this new radio, I'm remembering another new radio that lived in the past.

I think I was about twelve years old up in the Pacific Northwest where winter meant that it was always raining and muddy.

We had an old 1930s kind of radio that was in a huge cabinet that looked like a coffin and it scared me because old furniture can frighten children and make them think about dead people.

The radio was in pretty bad shape soundwise and it had become harder and harder to listen to my favorite programs on it.

The radio was beyond any kind of real repair job. It was holding onto a pathetic sound by the skin of its dial.

We had needed a new radio for a long while but we couldn't afford one because we were too poor. Finally we got enough money for the down payment to buy a radio on time and we walked over through the mud to the local radio store.

This was my mother and me and my sister and we all listened to brand-new radios as if we were in paradise until we had narrowed it down to the radio that we finally bought.

It was breathtakingly beautiful in a fine wooden cabinet that smelled like a lumberyard in heaven. The radio was a table model which was really nice, too.

We walked home with the radio down muddy streets that had no sidewalks. The radio was in a guarding cardboard box and I got to carry it. I felt so proud.

That was one of the happiest nights of my life listening to my favorite programs on a brand-new radio while a winter's rainstorm shook the house. Each program sounded as if it had been cut from a diamond. The hoof beats of the Cisco Kid's horse sparkled like a ring.

I'm sitting here now, baldingfatmiddleagedyearslater, listening to a talk show on the second brand-new radio of my life while shadows of the same storm shake the house.

I WAS TRYING
TO DESCRIBE YOU
TO SOMEONE

I was trying to describe you to someone a few days ago. You don't look like any girl I've ever seen before.

I couldn't say: "Well, she looks just like Jane Fonda except that she's got red hair and her mouth is different and of course she's not a movie star."

I couldn't say that because you don't look like Jane Fonda at all.

I finally ended up describing you as a movie I saw when I was a child in Tacoma, Washington. I guess I saw it in 1941 or '42: somewhere in there. I think I was seven or eight or six. It was a movie about rural electrification and a perfect 1930s New Deal morality kind of movie to show kids.

The movie was about farmers living in the country without electricity. They had to use lanterns to see by at night, for sewing and reading, and they didn't have any appliances, like toasters or washing machines, and they couldn't listen to the radio.

Then they built a dam with big electric generators and they

put poles across the countryside and strung wire over fields and pastures.

There was an incrédible heroic dimension that came from the simple putting up of poles for the wires to travel along. They looked ancient and modern at the same time.

Then the movie showed Electricity like a young Greek god coming to the farmer to take away forever the dark ways of his life.

Suddenly, religiously, with the throwing of a switch the farmer had electric lights to see by when he milked his cows in the early black winter mornings.

The farmer's family got to listen to the radio and have a toaster and lots of bright lights to sew dresses and read the newspaper by.

It was really a fantastic movie and excited me like listening to "The Star-Spangled Banner" or seeing photographs of President Roosevelt or hearing him on the radio.

". . . The President of the United States . . ."

I wanted electricity to go everywhere in the world. I wanted all the farmers in the world to be able to listen to President Roosevelt on the radio.

That's how you look to me.

TRICK OR TREATING
DOWN TO THE SEA
IN SHIPS

As a child I used to play at Halloween as if I were a sailor and go trick or treating down to the sea in ships. My sack of candy and things were at the wheel and my Halloween mask was sails cutting through a beautiful autumn night with lights on front porches shining like ports of call.

Trickortreat was the captain of our ship, saying, "We are only going to be in this port for a short time. I want all of you to go ashore and have a good time. Just remember we sail on the morning tide." My God, he was right! We sailed on the morning tide.

BLACKBERRY MOTORIST

THE blackberry vines grew all around and climbed like green dragon tails the sides of some old abandoned warehouses in an industrial area that had seen its day. The vines were so huge that people laid planks across them like bridges to get at the good berries in the center of them.

There were many bridges reaching into the vines. Some of them were five or six planks long and it took careful balancing to get back in there because if you fell off, there were nothing but blackberry vines for fifteen feet or so beneath you, and you could really hurt yourself on their thorns.

This was not a place you went casually to gather a few blackberries for a pie or to eat with some milk and sugar on them. You went there because you were getting blackberries for the winter's jam or to sell them because you needed more money than the price of a movie.

There were so many blackberries back in there that it was hard to believe. They were huge like black diamonds but it took a lot of medieval blackberry engineering, chopping entrances and laying bridges, to be successful like the siege of a castle.

"The castle has fallen!"

Sometimes when I got bored with picking blackberries I used to look into the deep shadowy dungeon-like places way down in the vines. You could see things that you couldn't make out down there and shapes that seemed to change like phantoms.

Once I was so curious that I crouched down on the fifth plank of a bridge that I had put together way out there in the vines and stared hard into the depths where thorns were like the spikes on a wicked mace until my eyes got used to the darkness and I saw a Model A sedan directly underneath me.

I crouched on that plank for a long time staring down at the car until I noticed that my legs were cramped. It took me about two hours to tunnel my way with ripped clothes and many bleeding scratches into the front seat of that car with my hands on the steering wheel, a foot on the gas pedal, a foot on the brake, surrounded by the smell of castle-like upholstery and staring from twilight darkness through the windshield up into green sunny shadows.

Some other blackberry pickers came along and started picking blackberries on the planks above me. They were very excited. I think it was the first time they had ever been there and seen blackberries like that. I sat there in the car underneath them and listened to them talk.

"Hey, look at this blackberry!"

THOREAU RUBBER BAND

LIFE is as simple as driving through New Mexico in a borrowed Jeep, sitting next to a girl who is so pretty that every time I look at her I just feel good all over. It's been snowing a lot and we've had to drive a hundred and fifty miles out of our way because the snow like an hourglass has closed the road that we needed.

Actually, I'm very excited because we are driving into the little town of Thoreau, New Mexico, to see if Highway 56 is open to Chaco Canyon. We want to see the Indian ruins there.

The ground is covered with snow so heavy that it looks as if it has just received its Government pension and is looking forward to a long and cheerful retirement.

We see a cafe resting in the snow's leisure. I get out of the Jeep and leave the girl sitting there while I go into the cafe to find out about the road.

The waitress is middle-aged. She looks at me as if I am a foreign movie that has just come in out of the snow starring

Jean-Paul Belmondo and Catherine Deneuve. The cafe smells like a fifty-foot-long breakfast. Two Indians are sitting at it, eating ham and eggs.

They are quiet and curious about me. They look at me sideways. I ask the waitress about the road and she tells me that it's closed. She says it in one quick final sentence. Well, that takes care of that.

I start out the door but one of the Indians turns and says sideways to me, "The road's open. I went over it this morning."

"Is it open all the way to Highway 44: the road over to Cuba?" I ask him.

"Yes."

The waitress suddenly turns her attention to the coffee. The coffee needs taking care of right now and that is what she is doing for the benefit of all the generations of coffee drinkers to come. Without her dedication, coffee might become extinct in Thoreau, New Mexico.

44:40

WHEN I knew Cameron he was a very old man and wore carpet slippers all the time and didn't talk any more. He smoked cigars and occasionally listened to Burl Ives' records. He lived with one of his sons who was now a middle-aged man himself and starting to complain about growing old.

"God-damn it, there's no getting around the fact that I'm not as young as I used to be."

Cameron had his own easy chair in the front room. It was covered with a wool blanket. Nobody else ever sat in that chair, but it was always as if he were sitting there, anyway. His spirit had taken command of that chair. Old people have a way of doing that with the furniture they end their lives sitting in.

He didn't go outside any more during the winter, but he would sit out on the front porch sometimes in the summer and stare past the rose bushes in the front yard to the street beyond where life calendared its days without him as if he had never existed out there at all.

That wasn't true, though. He used to be a great dancer and would dance all night long in the 1890s. He was famous for his dancing. He sent many a fiddler to an early grave and when the girls danced with him, they always danced better and they loved him for it and just the mention of his name in that county made the girls feel good and would get them blushing and giggling. Even the "serious" girls would get excited by his name or the sight of him.

There were a lot of broken hearts when he married the youngest of the Singleton girls in 1900.

"She's not that pretty," refrained the sore losers and they all cried at the wedding.

He was also a hell-of-a good poker player in a county where people played very serious poker for high stakes. Once a man sitting next to him was caught cheating during a game.

There was a lot of money on the table and a piece of paper that represented twelve head of cattle, two horses and a wagon. That was part of a bet.

The man's cheating was made public by one of the other men at the table reaching swiftly across without saying a word and cutting the man's throat.

Cameron automatically reached over and put his thumb on the man's jugular vein to keep the blood from getting all over the table and held him upright, though he was dying until the hand was finished and the ownership of the twelve head of cattle, two horses and a wagon was settled.

Though Cameron didn't talk any more, you could see events like that in his eyes. His hands had been made vegetable-like by rheumatism but there was an enormous dignity to their repose. The way he lit a cigar was like an act of history.

Once he had spent a winter as a sheepherder in 1889. He was a young man, not yet out of his teens. It was a long lonely winter job in God-forsaken country, but he needed the money to pay off a debt that he owed his father. It was one of those complicated family debts that it's best not to go into detail about.

There was very little exciting to do that winter except look at sheep but Cameron found something to keep his spirits up.

Ducks and geese flew up and down the river all winter and the man who owned the sheep had given him and the other sheepherders a lot, an almost surrealistic amount, of 44:40 Winchester ammunition to keep the wolves away, though there weren't any wolves in that country.

The owner of the sheep had a tremendous fear of wolves getting to his flock. It bordered on being ridiculous if you were to go by all the 44:40 ammunition he supplied his sheepherders.

Cameron heavily favored this ammunition with his rifle that winter by shooting at the ducks and geese from a hillside about two hundred yards from the river. A 44:40 isn't exactly the greatest bird gun in the world. It lets go with a huge slow-moving bullet like a fat man opening a door. Cameron wanted those kind of odds.

The long months of that family-debted-exile winter passed slowly day after day, shot after shot until it was finally spring and he had maybe fired a few thousand shots at those ducks and geese without hitting a single one of them.

Cameron loved to tell that story and thought it was very funny and always laughed during the telling. Cameron told that story just about as many times as he had fired at those birds years in front of and across the bridge of 1900 and up the decades of this century until he stopped talking.

PERFECT CALIFORNIA DAY

I was walking down the railroad tracks outside of Monterey on Labor Day in 1965, watching the Sierra shoreline of the Pacific Ocean. It has always been a constant marvel to me how much the ocean along there is like a high Sierra river with a granite shore and fiercely-clear water and turns of green and blue with chandelier foam shining in and out of the rocks like the currents of a river high in the mountains.

It's hard to believe that it's the ocean along there if you don't look up. Sometimes I like to think of that shore as a small river and carefully forget that it's 11,000 miles to the other bank.

I went around a bend in the river and there were a dozen or so frog people having a picnic on a sandy little beach surrounded by granite rocks. They were all in black rubber suits. They were standing in a circle eating big slices of watermelon. Two of them were pretty girls who wore soft felt hats on top of their suits.

The frog people were of course all talking frog people talk.

Often they were child-like and a summer of tadpole dialogue went by in the wind. Some of them had weird blue markings on the shoulders and down the arms of their suits like a brand-new blood system.

There were two German police dogs playing around the frog people. The dogs were not wearing black rubber suits and I did not see any suits lying on the beach for them. Perhaps their suits were behind a rock.

A frog man was floating on his back in the surf, eating a slice of watermelon. He swirled and eddied with the tide.

A lot of their equipment was leaning against a large theater-like rock that would have given Prometheus a run for his money. There were some yellow oxygen tanks lying next to the rock. They looked like flowers.

The frog people changed into a half-circle and then two of them ran into the sea and turned back to throw pieces of watermelon at the others and two of them started wrestling on the shore in the sand and the dogs were barking around them.

The girls were very pretty in their poured-on black rubber suits and gentle clowning hats. Eating watermelon, they sparkled like jewels in the crown of California.

THE POST OFFICES
OF EASTERN OREGON

DRIVING along in Eastern Oregon: autumn and the guns in the back seat and the shells in the jockey box or glove compartment, whatever you elect to call it.

I was just another kid going deer hunting in this land of mountains. We had come a long ways, leaving before it was dark. Then all night.

Now the sun was shining inside the car, hot like an insect, a bee or something, trapped and buzzing against the windshield.

I was very sleepy and asking Uncle Jarv, who was stuffed beside me in the front seat, about the country and the animals. I looked over at Uncle Jarv. He was driving and the steering wheel was awkwardly close in front of him. He weighed well over two hundred pounds. The car was barely enough room for him.

There in the half-light of sleep was Uncle Jarv, some Copenhagen in his mouth. It was always there. People used to like Copenhagen. There were signs all around telling you to buy some. You don't see those signs any more.

Uncle Jarv had once been a locally famous high school

athlete and later on, a legendary honky-tonker. He once had four hotel rooms at the same time and a bottle of whiskey in each room, but they had all left him. He had grown older.

Uncle Jarv lived quietly, reflectively now, reading Western novels and listening to opera on the radio every Saturday morning. He always had some Copenhagen in his mouth. The four hotel rooms and the four bottles of whiskey had vanished. Copenhagen had become his fate and his eternal condition.

I was just another kid pleasantly thinking about the two boxes of 30:30 shells in the jockey box. "Are there any mountain lions?" I asked.

"You mean cougars?" Uncle Jarv said.

"Yeah, cougars."

"Sure," Uncle Jarv said. His face was red and his hair was thin. He had never been a good-looking man but that had never stopped women from liking him. We kept crossing the same creek over and over again.

We crossed it at least a dozen times, and it was always a surprise to see the creek again because it was kind of pleasant, the water low with long months of heat, going through country that had been partially logged off.

"Are there any wolves?"

"A few. We're getting close to town now," Uncle Jarv said. We saw a farm house. Nobody lived there. It was abandoned like a musical instrument.

There was a good pile of wood beside the house. Do ghosts burn wood? I guess it's up to them, but the wood was the color of years.

"How about wildcats? There's a bounty on them, isn't there?"

We passed by a sawmill. There was a little log pond dammed up behind the creek. Two guys were standing on the logs. One of them had a lunch bucket in his hand.

"A few dollars," Uncle Jarv said.

We were now coming into the town. It was a small place. The houses and stores were rinky-tinky, and looked as if a lot of weather had been upon them.

"How about bears?" I said, just as we went around a bend in the road, and right in front of us was a pickup truck and there were two guys standing beside the truck, taking bears out of it.

"The country's filled with bears," Uncle Jarv said. "There are a couple of them right over there."

And sure enough . . . as if it were a plan, the guys were lifting the bears out, handling the bears as if they were huge pumpkins covered with long black hair. We stopped the car by the bears and got out.

There were people standing around looking at the bears. They were all old friends of Uncle Jarv's. They all said hello to Uncle Jarv, and where you been?

I had never heard so many people saying hello at once. Uncle Jarv had left the town many years before. "Hello, Jarv, hello." I expected the bears to say hello.

"Hello, Jarv, you old bad penny. What's that you're wearing around there for a belt? One of them Goodyears?"

"Ho-ho, let's take a look at the bears."

They were both cubs, weighing about fifty or sixty pounds. They had been shot up on Old Man Summers' Creek. The mother had gotten away. After the cubs were dead, she ran into a thicket, and hid in close with the ticks.

Old Man Summers' Creek! That's where we were going hunting. Up Old Man Summers' Creek! I'd never been there before. Bears!

"She'll be mean," one of the guys standing there said. We were going to stay at his house. He was the guy who shot the bears. He was a good friend of Uncle Jarv's. They had played together on the high school football team during the Depression.

A woman came by. She had a sack of groceries in her arms. She stopped and looked at the bears. She got up very close, leaning over toward the bears, shoving celery tops in their faces.

They took the bears and put them on the front porch of an old two-story house. The house had wooden frosting all around the edges. It was a birthday cake from a previous century. Like candles we were going to stay there for the night.

The trellis around the porch had some kind of strange-looking vines growing on it, with even stranger-looking flowers. I'd seen those vines and the flowers before, but never on a house. They were hops.

It was the first time that I had ever seen hops growing on a house. That was an interesting taste in flowers. But it took a little while to get used to them.

The sun was shining out front and the shadow of the hops lay across the bears as if they were two glasses of dark beer. They were sitting there, backs against the wall.

"Hello, gentlemen. What would you like to drink?"

"A couple of bears."

"I'll check the icebox and see if they're cold. I put some in there a little while ago . . . yeah, they're cold."

The guy who shot the bears decided that he didn't want them, so somebody said, "Why don't you give them to the mayor? He likes bears." The town had a population of three hundred and fifty-two, including the mayor and the bears.

"I'll go tell the mayor there are some bears over here for him," somebody said and went to find the mayor.

Oh, how good those bears would taste: roasted, fried, boiled or made into spaghetti, bear spaghetti just like the Italians make.

Somebody had seen him over at the sheriff's. That was about an hour ago. He might still be there. Uncle Jarv and I went over and had lunch at a little restaurant. The screen door was badly in need of repair, and opened like a rusty bicycle. The waitress asked us what we wanted. There were some slot machines by the door. The county was wide open.

We had some roast beef sandwiches with mashed potatoes and gravy. There were hundreds of flies in the place. Quite a crew of them had found some strips of flypaper that were hanging here and there like nooses in the restaurant, and were making themselves at home.

An old man came in. He said he wanted a glass of milk. The waitress got one for him. He drank it and put a nickel in a slot machine on his way out. Then he shook his head.

After we finished eating, Uncle Jarv had to go over to the post office and send a postcard. We walked over there and it was just a small building, more like a shack than anything else. We opened the screen door and went in.

There was a lot of post office stuff: a counter and an old clock with a long drooping hand like a mustache under the sea, swinging softly back and forth, keeping time with time.

There was a large nude photograph of Marilyn Monroe on the wall. The first one I had ever seen in a post office. She was lying on a big piece of red. It seemed like a strange thing to have on the wall of a post office, but of course I was a stranger in the land.

The postmistress was a middle-aged woman, and she had copied on her face one of those mouths they used to wear during the 1920s. Uncle Jarv bought a postcard and filled it up on the counter as if it were a glass of water.

It took a couple of moments. Halfway through the postcard
Uncle Jarv stopped and glanced up at Marilyn Monroe. There
was nothing lustful about his looking up there. She just as
well could have been a photograph of mountains and trees.

I don't remember whom he was writing to. Perhaps it was
to a friend or a relative. I stood there staring at the nude photograph of Marilyn Monroe for all I was worth. Then Uncle
Jarv mailed the postcard. "Come on," he said.

We went back to the house where the bears were, but they
were gone. "Where did they go?" somebody said.

A lot of people had gathered around and they were all
talking about the missing bears and were kind of looking for
the bears all over the place.

"They're dead," somebody said, trying to be reassuring,
and pretty soon we were looking inside the house, and a
woman went through the closets, looking for bears.

After a while the mayor came over and said, "I'm hungry.
Where are my bears?"

Somebody told the mayor that they had disappeared into
thin air and the mayor said, "That's impossible," and got down
and looked under the porch. There were no bears there.

An hour or so passed and everybody gave up looking for
the bears, and the sun went down. We sat outside on the front
porch where once upon a time, there had been bears.

The men talked about playing high school football during
the Depression, and made jokes about how old and fat they
had grown. Somebody asked Uncle Jarv about the four hotel
rooms and the four bottles of whiskey. Everybody laughed
except Uncle Jarv. He smiled instead. Night had just started
when somebody found the bears.

They were on a side street sitting in the front seat of a car.
One of the bears had on a pair of pants and a checkered shirt.
He was wearing a red hunting hat and had a pipe in the

mouth and two paws on the steering wheel like Barney Old-
field.

The other bear had on a white silk negligee, one of the kind
you see advertised in the back pages of men's magazines, and
a pair of felt slippers stuck on the feet. There was a pink
bonnet tied on the head and a purse in the lap.

Somebody opened up the purse, but there wasn't anything
inside. I don't know what they expected to find, but they
were disappointed. What would a dead bear carry in its purse,
anyway?

★   ★   ★

Strange is the thing that makes me recall all this again: the
bears. It's a photograph in the newspaper of Marilyn Monroe,
dead from a sleeping pill suicide, young and beautiful, as they
say, with everything to live for.

The newspapers are filled with it: articles and photographs
and the like—her body being taken away on a cart, the body
wrapped in a dull blanket. I wonder what post office wall in
Eastern Oregon will wear this photograph of Marilyn Monroe.

An attendant is pushing the cart out a door, and the sun is
shining under the cart. Venetian blinds are in the photograph
and the branches of a tree.

PALE MARBLE MOVIE

THE room had a high Victorian ceiling and there was a marble fireplace and an avocado tree growing in the window, and she lay beside me sleeping in a very well-built blond way.

And I was asleep, too, and it was just starting to be dawn in September.

1964.

Then suddenly, without any warning, she sat up in bed, waking me instantly, and she started to get out of bed. She was very serious about it.

"What are you doing?" I said.

Her eyes were wide open.

"I'm getting up," she said.

They were a somnambulist blue.

"Get back in bed," I said.

"Why?" she said, now halfway out of bed with one blond foot touching the floor.

"Because you're still asleep," I said.

"Ohhh . . . OK," she said. That made sense to her and

she got back into bed and pulled the covers around herself and cuddled up close to me. She didn't say another word and she didn't move.

She lay there sound asleep with her wanderings over and mine just beginning. I have been thinking about this simple event for years now. It stays with me and repeats itself over and over again like a pale marble movie.

PARTNERS

I like to sit in the cheap theaters of America where people live and die with Elizabethan manners while watching the movies. There is a theater down on Market Street where I can see four movies for a dollar. I really don't care how good they are either. I'm not a critic. I just like to watch movies. Their presence on the screen is enough for me.

The theater is filled with black people, hippies, senior citizens, soldiers, sailors and the innocent people who talk to the movies because the movies are just as real as anything else that has ever happened to them.

"No! No! Get back in the car, Clyde. Oh, God, they're killing Bonnie!"

I am the poet-in-residence at these theaters but I don't plan on getting a Guggenheim for it.

Once I went into the theater at six o'clock in the evening and got out at one o'clock in the morning. At seven I crossed my legs and they stayed that way until ten and I never did stand up.

In other words, I am not an art film fan. I do not care to be esthetically tickled in a fancy theater surrounded by an audience drenched in the confident perfume of culture. I can't afford it.

I was sitting in a two-pictures-for-seventy-five-cents theater called the Times in North Beach last month and there was a cartoon about a chicken and a dog.

The dog was trying to get some sleep and the chicken was keeping him awake and what followed was a series of adventures that always ended up in cartoon mayhem.

There was a man sitting next to me.

He was WHITEWHITEWHITE: fat, about fifty years old, balding sort of and his face was completely minus any human sensitivity.

His baggy no-style clothes covered him like the banner of a defeated country and he looked as if the only mail he had ever gotten in his life were bills.

Just then the dog in the cartoon let go with a huge yawn because the chicken was still keeping him awake and before the dog had finished yawning, the man next to me started yawning, so that the dog in the cartoon and the man, this living human being, were yawning together, partners in America.

GETTING TO KNOW
EACH OTHER

SHE hates hotel rooms. It's like a Shakespearean sonnet. I mean, the childwoman or Lolita thing. It's a classic form:

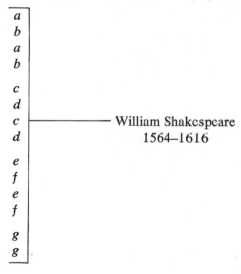

a
b
a
b

c
d
c
d

e
f
e
f

g
g

———————— William Shakespeare
1564–1616

She hates hotel rooms. It's the light in the morning that really bothers her. She doesn't like to wake up surrounded by that kind of light.

The morning light in hotel rooms is always synthetic, harshly clean as if the maid had let herself so quietly in, like a maidmouse, and put the light there by making phantom beds with strange sheets hanging in the very air itself.

She used to lie in bed and pretend that she was still asleep, so as to catch the maid coming in with the morning light folded in her arms, but she never caught her and finally gave it up.

Her father is asleep in the other room with a new lover. Her father is a famous movie director and in town to promote one of his pictures.

This trip to San Francisco he is promoting a horror movie that he has just finished directing called *The Attack of the Giant Rose People*. It is a film about a mad gardener and the results of his handiwork in the greenhouse working with experimental fertilizers.

She thinks the giant rose people are a bore. "They look like a bunch of funky valentines," she recently told her father.

"Why don't you go fuck yourself?" had been his reply.

That afternoon he would have lunch with Paine Knickerbocker of the *Chronicle* and later on in the afternoon he would be interviewed by Eichelbaum of the *Examiner* and a few days later her father's same old line of bullshit would appear in the papers.

Last night he rented a suite at the Fairmont but she wanted to stay at a motel on Lombard.

"Are you crazy? This is San Francisco!" he'd said.

She likes motels a lot better than she does hotels, but she doesn't know why. Maybe it's the light in the morning. That probably has something to do with it. The light in motel rooms is more natural. It's not as if the maid had put it there.

She got out of bed. She wanted to see who her father was sleeping with. It was a little game of hers. She liked to see if she could guess who her father was in bed with, but it was a kind of silly game and she knew it because the women that her father went to bed with always looked just like her.

She wondered where her father kept finding them.

Some of his friends and other people liked to make little jokes about it. They liked to say that his lovers and his daughter always looked like sisters. Sometimes she felt as if she were the member of a strange and changing family of sisters.

She was 5-7, had straight blond hair that went almost down to her ass. She weighed 113 pounds. She had *very* blue eyes.

She was fifteen years old but she could have been any age. With just the turn of a whim she could look anywhere between thirteen and thirty-five.

Sometimes she would deliberately look thirty-five, so that young men in their early twenties would be attracted to her and consider her to be an older, experienced woman.

She could perform perfectly the role of a still glamorous but fading thirty-five-year-old woman, having studied so many of them in Hollywood, New York, Paris, Rome, London, etc.

She'd already had three affairs with young men in their early twenties without them ever catching on that she was only fifteen.

It had become a little hobby of hers.

She could invent whole lifetimes for herself and it was as if she had lived them in a kind of dreamy telescope way. She could be a thirty-four-year-old matron with three children in Glendale married to a Jewish dentist and having a lost youth fling on the side or she could be a thirty-one-year-old spinster literary editor from New York trying to escape the clutches of an insane lesbian lover and needing a young man to provide her salvation from perversion or she could be a thirty-year-old divorcée with an incurable but attractive disease and wanting to have one more chance at romance before . . .

She loved it.

She got out of bed and tiptoed without any clothes on into the living room and went over to the door of her father's bedroom and stood there listening to see if they were awake or making love.

Her father and his lover were sound asleep. She could feel it through the door. It was like a chunk of warm frozen space in their bedroom.

She opened the door a crack and saw the blond hair of the woman spilling over the side of the bed like the sleeve of a yellow shirt.

She smiled and closed the door.

And that's where we leave her.

We know a little about her.

And she knows a lot about us.

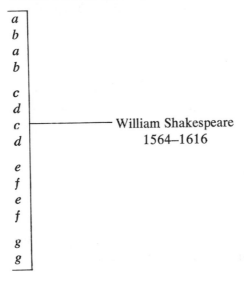

a
b
a
b

c
d
c ———————— William Shakespeare
d 1564–1616

e
f
e
f

g
g

A SHORT HISTORY
OF OREGON

I would do things like that when I was sixteen. I'd hitch-hike
fifty miles in the rain to go hunting for the last hours of the
day. I'd stand alongside the road with a 30:30 and my thumb
out and think nothing of it, expecting to be picked up and I
always was.

"Where are you going?"

"Deer hunting."

That meant something in Oregon.

"Get in."

It was raining like hell when I got out of the car at the top
of the ridge. The driver couldn't believe it. I saw a draw half-
full of trees, sloping down into a valley obscured by rain mist.

I hadn't the slightest idea where the valley led to. I'd never
been there before and I didn't care.

"Where are you going?" the driver said, hardly believing
that I was getting out of the car in the rain.

"Down there."

When he drove off I was alone in the mountains and that

was how I wanted it to be. I was waterproofed from head to toe and had some candy bars in my pocket.

I walked down through the trees, trying to kick a deer out of the dry thickets, but it didn't really make any difference if I saw one or not.

I just wanted the awareness of hunting. The thought of the deer being there was just as good as the deer actually being there.

There was nothing stirring in the thickets. I didn't see any sign of a deer or the sign of a bird or the sign of a rabbit or anything.

Sometimes I would just stand there. The trees were dripping. There was only the sign of myself: alone, so I ate a candy bar.

I had no idea of the time. The sky was dark with winter rain. I only had a couple of hours when I started and I could feel that they were nearly at an end and soon it would be night.

I came out of a thicket into a patch of stumps and a logging road that curved down into the valley. They were new stumps. The trees had been cut sometime that year. Perhaps in the spring. The road curved into the valley.

The rain slackened off, then stopped and a strange kind of silence settled over everything. It was twilight and wouldn't last long.

There was a turn in the logging road and suddenly, without warning, there was a house right there in the middle of my private nowhere. I didn't like it.

The house was more of a large shack than anything else with a lot of old cars surrounding it and there was all sorts of logging junk and things that you need and then abandon after using.

I didn't want the house to be there. The rain mist lifted and I looked back up the mountain. I'd come down only about half a mile, thinking all the time I was alone.

That was a joke.

There was a window in the house-shack facing up the road toward me. I couldn't see anything in the window. Even though it was starting to get night, they hadn't turned their lights on yet. I knew there was somebody home because heavy black smoke was coming out of the chimney.

As I got closer to the house, the front door slammed open and a kid ran out onto a crude makeshift porch. He didn't have any shoes or a coat on. He was about nine years old and his blond hair was disheveled as if the wind were blowing all the time in his hair.

He looked older than nine and was immediately joined by three sisters who were three, five and seven. The sisters weren't wearing any shoes either and they didn't have any coats on. The sisters looked older than they were.

The quiet spell of the twilight broke suddenly and it started raining again, but the kids didn't go into the house. They just stood there on the porch, getting all wet and looking at me.

I'll have to admit that I was a strange sight coming down their muddy little road in the middle of God-damn nowhere with darkness coming on and a 30:30 cradled down in my arms, so the night rain wouldn't get in the barrel.

The kids didn't say a word as I walked by. The sisters' hair was unruly like dwarf witches'. I didn't see their folks. There was no light on in the house.

A Model A truck lay on its side in front of the house. It was next to three empty fifty-gallon oil drums. They didn't have a purpose any more. There were some odd pieces of rusty cable. A yellow dog came out and stared at me.

I didn't say a word in my passing. The kids were soaking wet now. They huddled together in silence on the porch. I had no reason to believe that there was anything more to life than this.

A LONG TIME AGO
PEOPLE DECIDED TO
LIVE IN AMERICA

I'M wandering along, thinking about how I'd like to get laid by somebody new. It's a cold winter afternoon and just another thought, almost out of my mind when—

A tall, God-I-love the tall-ones girl comes walking up the street, casual as a young animal with Levi's on. She must be 5-9, wearing a blue sweater. Her breasts are loose beneath it and move in firm youthful tide.

She has no shoes on.

She's a hippie girl.

Her hair is long.

She doesn't know how pretty she is. I like that. It always turns me on, which isn't very hard to do right now because I'm already thinking about girls.

Then as we pass each other she turns toward me, a thing totally unexpected and she says, "Don't I know you?"

Wow! She is standing beside me now. She's really tall!

I look closely at her. I try to see if I know her. Maybe she's a former lover or somebody else I've met or made a pass at when I've been drunk. I look carefully at her and she is beautiful in a fresh young way. She has the nicest blue eyes, but I don't recognize her.

"I know I've seen you before," she says, looking up into my face. "What's your name?"

"Clarence."

"Clarence?"

"Yeah, Clarence."

"Oh, then I don't know you," she says.

That was kind of fast.

Her feet are cold on the pavement and she's hunched in a cold-like way toward me.

"What is your name?" I ask, maybe I'm going to make a pass at her. That's what I should be doing right now. Actually, I'm about thirty seconds late in doing it.

"Willow Woman," she says. "I'm trying to get out to the Haight-Ashbury. I just got into town from Spokane."

"I wouldn't," I say. "It's very bad out there."

"I have friends in the Haight-Ashbury," she says.

"It's a bad place," I say.

She shrugs her shoulders and looks helplessly down at her feet. Then she looks up and her eyes have a friendly wounded expression in them.

"This is all I have," she says.

(Meaning what she is wearing.)

"And what's in my pocket," she says.

(Her eyes glance furtively toward the left rear pocket of her Levi's.)

"My friends will help me out when I get there," she says.

(Glancing in the direction of the Haight-Ashbury three miles away.)

Suddenly she has become awkward. She doesn't know exactly what to do. She has taken two steps backward. They are in the direction of going up the street.

"I . . . ," she says.

"I . . . ," looking down at her cold feet again.

She takes another half-step backward.

"I."

"I don't want to whine," she says.

She's really disgusted with what's happening now. She's ready to leave. It didn't work out the way she wanted.

"Let me help you," I say.

I reach into my pocket.

She steps toward me, instantly relieved as if a miracle has happened.

I give her a dollar, having totally lost somewhere the thread of making a pass at her, which I had planned on doing.

She can't believe it's a dollar and throws her arms around me and kisses me on the cheek. Her body is warm, friendly and giving.

We could make a nice scene together. I could say the words that would cause it to be, but I don't say anything because I've lost the thread of making a pass at her and don't know where it's gone, and she departs beautifully toward all the people that she will ever meet, at best I will turn out to be a phantom memory, and all the lives that she will live.

We've finished living this one together.

She's gone.

A SHORT HISTORY
OF RELIGION
IN CALIFORNIA

THERE'S only one way to get into it: We saw the deer in the meadow. The deer turned in a slow circle and then broke the circle and went toward some trees.

There were three deer in the meadow and we were three people. I, a friend and my daughter 3½ years old. "See the deer," I said, pointing the way to the deer.

"Look the deer! There! There!" she said and surged against me as I held her in the front seat. A little jolt of electricity had come to her from the deer. Three little gray dams went away into the trees, celebrating a TVA of hoofs.

She talked about the deer as we drove back to our camp in Yosemite. "Those deer are really something," she said. "I'd like to be a deer."

When we turned into our campground there were three deer standing at the entrance, looking at us. They were the same deer or they were three different ones.

"Look the deer!" and the same electrical surge against me, enough perhaps to light a couple of Christmas tree lights or make a fan turn for a minute or toast half a slice of bread.

The deer followed close behind the car as we drove at deer speed into the camp. When we got out of the car, the deer were there. My daughter took out after them. Wow! The deer!

I slowed her down. "Wait," I said. "Let Daddy take your hand." I didn't want her to scare them or get hurt by them either, in case they should panic and run over her, a next to impossible thing.

We followed after the deer, a little ways behind and then stopped to watch them cross the river. The river was shallow and the deer stopped in the middle and looked in three different directions.

She stared at them, not saying anything for a while. How quiet and beautiful they looked and then she said, "Daddy, take off the deer's head and put it on my head. Take off the deer's feet, put them on my feet. And I'll be the deer."

The deer stopped looking in three different directions. They all looked in one direction toward the trees on the other side of the river and moved off into those trees.

So the next morning there was a band of Christians camping beside us because it was Sunday. There were about twenty or thirty of them seated at a long wooden table. They were singing hymns while we were taking down our tent.

My daughter watched them very carefully and then walked over to peek out at them from behind a tree as they sang on. There was a man leading them. He waved his hands in the air. Probably their minister.

My daughter watched them very carefully and then moved out from behind the tree and slowly advanced until she was right behind their minister, looking up at him. He was standing out there alone and she was standing out there alone with him.

I pulled the metal tent stakes out of the ground and put them together in a neat pile, and I folded the tent and put it beside the tent stakes.

Then one of the Christian women got up from the long table and walked over to my daughter. I was watching this. She gave her a piece of cake and asked her if she wanted to sit down and listen to the singing. They were busy singing something about Jesus doing something good for them.

My daughter nodded her head and sat down on the ground. She held the piece of cake in her lap. She sat there for five minutes. She did not take a bite out of the piece of cake.

They were now singing about Mary and Joseph doing something. In the song it was winter and cold and there was straw in the barn. It smelled good.

She listened for about five minutes and then she got up, waved good-bye in the middle of "We Three Kings of Orient Are" and came back with the piece of cake.

"Well, how was that?" I said.

"Singing," she said, pointing they are singing.

"How's the cake?" I said.

"I don't know," she said and threw it on the ground. "I've already had breakfast." It lay there.

I thought about the three deer and the Christians singing. I looked at the piece of cake and to the river where the deer had been gone for a day.

The cake was very small on the ground. The water flowed over the rocks. A bird or an animal would eat the cake later on and then go down to the river for a drink of water.

A little thing came to my mind and having no other choice: it pleased me, so I hugged my arms around a tree and my cheek sailed to the sweet bark and floated there for a few gentle moments in the calm.

APRIL IN GOD-DAMN

THIS early April in God-damn God-damn begins with a note on the front door, left by a young lady. I read the note and wonder what the hell's up.

I'm too old for this kind of stuff. I can't keep track of everything, and so I go pick up my daughter and do the best I can on that front: take her to play in the park.

I really don't want to get out of bed, but I have to go to the toilet. Returning from the toilet, I see something a note or something fastened to the glass window on the front door. It leaves a shadow on the glass.

I don't give a damn. Let somebody else handle these complicated things in early April. It's enough for me to have gone to the toilet. I go back to bed.

I dream that somebody I don't like is walking their dog. The dream takes hours. The person is singing to their dog but I can't make out what the song is and I have to listen too hard and never get it, anyway.

I wake up totally bored. What am I going to do with the

rest of my life? I'm twenty-nine. I get the note off the door and go back to bed.

I read it with the sheet pulled up over my head. The light is not very good but it is better than anything else I've come across today. It's from a girl. She came by so quietly this morning and left it on my door.

The note is an apology for a bad scene she made the other night. It is in the form of a riddle. I can't figure it out. I never cared for riddles, anyway. Fuck her.

I go get my daughter and take her to the playground at Portsmouth Square. I have been watching her for the last hour. From time to time I have paused to write this down.

I wonder if my daughter will ever leave a note on some man's door in early April God-damn God-damn and he'll read it in bed with the sheet pulled up over his head and then take his daughter to the park and look up as I just did to see her playing with a blue bucket in the sand.

ONE AFTERNOON
IN 1939

THIS is a constant story that I keep telling my daughter who is four years old. She gets something from it and wants to hear it again and again.

When it's time for her to go to bed, she says, "Daddy, tell me about when you were a kid and climbed inside that rock."

"OK."

She cuddles the covers about her as if they were controllable clouds and puts her thumb in her mouth and looks at me with listening blue eyes.

"Once when I was a little kid, just your age, my mother and father took me on a picnic to Mount Rainier. We drove up there in an old car and saw a deer standing in the middle of the road.

"We came to a meadow where there was snow in the shadows of the trees and snow in the places where the sun didn't shine.

"There were wild flowers growing in the meadow and they looked beautiful. In the middle of the meadow there was a huge round rock and Daddy walked over to the rock and found a hole in the center of it and looked inside. The rock was hollow like a small room.

"Daddy crawled inside the rock and sat there staring out at the blue sky and the wild flowers. Daddy really liked that rock and pretended that it was a house and he played inside the rock all afternoon.

"He got some smaller rocks and took them inside the big rock. He pretended that the smaller rocks were a stove and furniture and things and he cooked a meal, using wild flowers for food."

That's the end of the story.

Then she looks up at me with her deep blue eyes and sees me as a child playing inside a rock, pretending that wild flowers are hamburgers and cooking them on a small stove-like rock.

She can never get enough of this story. She has heard it thirty or forty times and always wants to hear it again.

It's very important to her.

I think she uses this story as a kind of Christopher Columbus door to the discovery of her father when he was a child and her contemporary.

CORPORAL

ONCE I had visions of being a general. This was in Tacoma during the early years of World War II when I was a child going to grade school. They had a huge paper drive that was brilliantly put together like a military career.

It was very exciting and went something like this: If you brought in fifty pounds of paper you became a private and seventy-five pounds of paper were worth a corporal's stripes and a hundred pounds to be a sergeant, then spiralling pounds of paper leading upward until finally you arrived at being a general.

I think it took a ton of paper to be a general or maybe it was only a thousand pounds. I can't remember the exact amount but in the beginning it seemed so simple to gather enough paper to be a general.

I started out by gathering all the loose paper that was lying innocently around the house. That added up to three or four pounds. I'll have to admit that I was a little disappointed. I don't know where I got the idea that the house was just filled with paper. I actually thought there was paper all over the place. It's an interesting surprise that paper can be deceptive.

I didn't let it throw me, though. I marshalled my energies and went out and started going door to door asking people if they had any newspapers or magazines lying around that could be donated to the paper drive, so that we could win the war and destroy evil forever.

An old woman listened patiently to my spiel and then she gave me a copy of *Life* magazine that she had just finished reading. She closed the door while I was still standing there staring dumbfoundedly at the magazine in my hands. The magazine was warm.

At the next house, there wasn't any paper, not even a used envelope because another kid had already beaten me to it.

At the next house, nobody was home.

That's how it went for a week, door after door, house after house, block after block until finally I got enough paper together to become a private.

I took my God-damn little private's stripe home in the absolute bottom of my pocket. There were already some paper officers, lieutenants and captains, on the block. I didn't even bother to have the stripe sewed on my coat. I just threw it in a drawer and covered it up with some socks.

I spent the next few days cynically looking for paper and lucked into a medium pile of *Collier's* from somebody's basement which was enough to get my corporal's stripes that immediately joined my private's stripe under the socks.

The kids who wore the best clothes and had a lot of spending money and got to eat hot lunch every day were already generals. They had known where there were a lot of magazines and their parents had cars. They strutted military airs around the playground and on their way home from school.

Shortly after that, like the next day, I brought a halt to my glorious military career and entered into the disenchanted paper shadows of America where failure is a bounced check or a bad report card or a letter ending a love affair and all the words that hurt people when they read them.

LINT

I'M haunted a little this evening by feelings that have no vo-
cabulary and events that should be explained in dimensions
of lint rather than words.

I've been examining half-scraps of my childhood. They are
pieces of distant life that have no form or meaning. They are
things that just happened like lint.

A COMPLETE HISTORY
OF GERMANY AND JAPAN

A few years ago (World War II) I lived in a motel next to a Swift packing plant which is a nice way of saying slaughter-house.

They killed pigs there, hour after hour, day after day, week after week, month after month until spring became summer and summer became fall, by cutting their throats after which would follow a squealing lament equal to an opera being run through a garbage disposal.

Somehow I thought that killing all those pigs had something to do with winning the war. I guess that was because everything else did.

For the first week or two that we lived in the motel it really bothered me. All that screaming was hard to take, but then I grew used to it and it became like any other sound: a bird singing in a tree or the noon whistle or the radio or trucks driving by or human voices or being called for dinner, etc.

"You can play after dinner!"

Whenever the pigs weren't screaming, the silence sounded as if a machine had broken down.

THE AUCTION

IT was a rainy Pacific Northwest auction with kids running all over the place getting into things and farm women interested in buying boxes of used fruit jars, secondhand dresses, and perhaps some furniture for the house while the men were interested in saddles and farm equipment and livestock.

The auction was in a kind of old warehousebarn-like building with used excitement everywhere on Saturday afternoon. It smelled like the complete history of America.

The auctioneer was selling things so fast that it was possible to buy stuff that wouldn't be for sale until next year. He had false teeth that sounded like crickets jumping up and down inside the jaws of a skeleton.

Whenever there was a box of old toys put up for auction, the kids would bother the hell out of their folks until they were threatened with the strap if they didn't shut up, "Stop pestering me or you won't be able to sit down for a week."

There were always cows and sheep, horses and rabbits

waiting to get new owners or a farmer somberly contemplating some chickens while blowing his nose.

It was great on a rainy winter afternoon because the auction had a tin roof and there was a beautiful wet closeness to everything inside.

An ancient case made out of dusty glass and long yellow wood like a pioneer's mustache contained boxes of stale candy bars. They were fifty cents a box and really stale but for some kid reason I liked to gnaw away on them and would work up a quarter and find somebody to go in with me on a box and I'd end up with twelve stale candy bars in 1947.

THE ARMORED CAR
For Janice

I lived in a room that had a bed and a telephone. That was all. One morning I was lying in bed and the telephone rang. The window shades were pulled down and it was raining hard outside. It was still dark.

"Hello," I said.

"Who invented the revolver?" a man asked.

Before I could hang the telephone up my own voice escaped me like an anarchist and said, "Samuel Colt."

"You just won a cord of wood," the man said.

"Who are you?" I asked.

"This is a contest," he said. "You just won a cord of wood."

"I don't have a stove," I said. "I live in a rented room. There's no heat."

"Is there anything else you would want besides a cord of wood?" he said.

"Yeah, a fountain pen."

"Good, we'll send you one. What's the address there?"

I gave him my address and then I asked him who was sponsoring the contest.

"Never mind," he said. "The pen will be in the mail tomorrow morning. Oh, yes, is there any particular color you like? I almost forgot."

"Blue would be fine."

"We're all out of blue. Any other color? Green? We have a lot of green pens."

"All right, green, then."

"It'll be in the mail tomorrow morning," he said.

It wasn't. It never came.

The only thing I ever won in my life and actually received was an armored car. When I was a child I had a paper route that went for miles along the rough edge of town.

I would have to ride my bicycle down a hill, following a road that had fields of grass on both sides and an old plum orchard at the end of the road. They had chopped down part of the trees and built four new houses there.

Parked in front of one house was an armored car. It was a small town and every day after work the driver took the armored car home with him. He parked it out in front of his house.

I would pass there before six o'clock in the morning and everybody would be asleep in the houses. When there was light in the morning I could see the armored car from a quarter of a mile or so.

I liked the armored car and would get off my bicycle and walk over and take a look at it, knock on the heavy metal, look in the bulletproof windows, kick the tires.

Because everybody was asleep in the morning and I alone out there, after a while I considered the armored car to be mine and treated it as such.

One morning I got into the armored car and delivered the

rest of my papers from it. It looked kind of strange to see a kid delivering newspapers from an armored car.

I rather enjoyed it and started doing it regularly.

"Here comes that kid in the armored car delivering papers," the early risers said. "Yeah, he's a nut."

That was the only thing I ever won.

THE LITERARY LIFE
IN CALIFORNIA/1964

1

I was sitting in a bar last night talking to a friend who was from time to time looking down the bar at his wife. They had been separated for two years: no hope.

She was palling it up with another man. They looked as if they were having a lot of fun.

My friend turned and asked me about two books of my poetry. I'm a minor poet, even so, people sometimes ask me questions like that.

He said he used to have the books but he didn't have them any more. They were gone. I said that one of the books was out of print and copies of the other book were down at City Lights Bookstore.

He took a look down at his wife. She was laughing at something the other man had said, who was then quite pleased with himself, and so it goes.

"I have a confession to make," my friend said. "Remember that night I came home from work and found you and my wife drunk together on sweet vermouth in the kitchen?"

I remembered the evening, though nothing had happened. We were just sitting there in the kitchen, listening to the phonograph and drunk on sweet vermouth. There were probably thousands like us all across America.

"Well, when you left I went and got those two books of poetry out of the bookcase and tore them up and threw the pieces on the floor. All the king's horses and all the king's men couldn't have put those books of poetry back together again."

"Win a few, lose a few," I said.

"What?" he said.

He was a little drunk. There were three empty beer bottles in front of him on the bar. Their labels had been carefully scratched off.

"I just write the poetry," I said. "I'm not a shepherd of the pages. I can't look after them forever. It wouldn't make sense."

I was also a little drunk.

"Anyway," my friend said. "I would like to have those books again. Where can I get them?"

"One of them has been out of print for five years. The other one you can get at City Lights," I said, busy putting together and filming in my mind what went on after I left the kitchen and went home, glowing like a lantern in sweet vermouth.

What he said to her before he went and got the books of poetry and tore them up. What she said, what he said, which book went first, the way he tore it. Oh, a lovely act of healthy outrage and what was taken care of after that.

2

I was at City Lights a year ago and saw somebody looking at one of my books of poetry. He was pleased with the book, but there was a reluctance to his pleasure.

He looked at the cover again and turned the pages again. He stopped the pages as if they were the hands of a clock and he was pleased at what time it was. He read a poem at seven o'clock in the book. Then the reluctance came again and clouded up the time.

He put the book back on the shelf, then he took it off the shelf. His reluctance had become a form of nervous energy.

Finally he reached in his pocket and took out a penny. He placed the book in the crook of his arm. The book was now a nest and the poems were eggs. He threw the penny up in the air, caught it and slapped it on the back of his hand. He took his other hand away.

He put the book of poetry back on the shelf and left the bookstore. As he walked out he looked very relaxed. I walked over and found his reluctance lying there on the floor.

It was like clay but nervous and fidgeting. I put it in my pocket. I took it home with me and shaped it into this, having nothing better to do with my time.

BANNERS OF MY
OWN CHOOSING

DRUNK laid and drunk unlaid and drunk laid again, it makes no difference. I return to this story as one who has been away but one who was always destined to return and perhaps that's for the best.

I found no statues nor bouquets of flowers, no beloved to say: "Now we will fly new banners from the castle, and they will be of your own choosing," and to hold my hand again, to take my hand in yours.

None of that stuff for me.

My typewriter is fast enough as if it were a horse that's just escaped from the ether, plunging through silence, and the words gallop in order while outside the sun is shining.

Perhaps the words remember me.

It is the fourth day of March 1964. The birds are singing on the back porch, a bunch of them in an aviary, and I try to sing with them: Drunk laid and drunk unlaid and drunk laid again, I'm back in town.

FAME
IN CALIFORNIA/1964

1

IT's really something to have fame put its feathery crowbar under your rock and then upward to the light release you, along with seven grubs and a sow bug.

I'll show you what happens, then. A friend of mine came up to me a few months ago and said, "You're a character in the novel I just finished."

It really set me up when he said that. I had an immediate vision of myself as the romantic lead or the villain: "He put his hand on her breast and his hot breath fogged up her glasses," or "He laughed as she cried, then he kicked her down the stairs like a sack of dirty laundry."

"What do I do in your novel?" I said, waiting to hear great words.

"You open a door," he said.

"What else do I do?"

"That's all."

"Oh," I said, my fame diminishing. "Couldn't I have done

something else? Maybe opened two doors? Kissed some-body?"

"That one door was enough," he said. "You were perfect."

"Did I say anything when I opened the door?" still hoping a little.

"No."

2

I met a photographer friend of mine last week. We were making the rounds of the bars. He took some photographs. He is a careful young photographer and conceals his camera under his coat like a pistol.

He doesn't want people to know what he is doing. Wants to capture them in real life poses. Doesn't want to make them nervous and begin acting like movie stars.

Then he whips out his camera like the bank robber that got away: that simple Indiana boy that's now living in Switzerland among royalty and big business and who has culti-vated a foreign accent.

Yesterday I met the young photographer and he had some large prints of the photographs he had taken that night.

"I took a picture of you," he said. "I'll show it to you."

He showed me through a dozen or so prints and then he turned to the next one and said, "See!" It was the photograph of an old woman drinking a rather silly martini.

"There you are," he said.

"Where?" I said. "I'm not an old woman."

"Of course not," he said. "That's your hand on the table."

I looked very carefully into the photograph and sure enough, but now I wonder what happened to the seven grubs and the sow bug.

I hope they made out a little better than I did after that

feathery crowbar lifted us to the light. Perhaps they have their own television show and are coming out with an LP and are having their novels published by Viking, and *Time* will ask them about themselves, "Just tell us how you got started. In your own words."

MEMORY OF A GIRL

I cannot look at the Fireman's Fund Insurance Company building without thinking of her breasts. The building is at Presidio and California Streets in San Francisco. It is a red brick, blue and glass building that looks like a minor philosophy plopped right down on the site of what was once one of California's most famous cemeteries:

Laurel Hill Cemetery
1854–1946

Eleven United States Senators were buried there.

They, and everybody else were moved out years ago, but there are still some tall cypress trees standing beside the insurance company.

These trees once cast their shadows over graves. They

were a part of daytime weeping and mourning, and nighttime silence except for the wind.

I wonder if they ask themselves questions like: Where did everybody go who was dead? Where did they take them? And where are those who came here to visit them? Why were we left behind?

Perhaps these questions are too poetic. Maybe it would be best just to say: There are four trees standing beside an insurance company out in California.

SEPTEMBER CALIFORNIA

SEPTEMBER 22 means that she is lying on the beach in a black bathing suit and she is very carefully taking her own temperature.

She is beautiful: long and white and obviously a secretary from Montgomery Street who went to San Jose State College for three years and this is not the first time that she has taken her own temperature in a black bathing suit at the beach.

She seems to be enjoying herself and I cannot take my eyes off her. Beyond the thermometer is a ship passing out of San Francisco Bay, bound for cities on the other side of the world, those places.

Her hair is the same color as the ship. I can almost see the captain. He is saying something to one of the crew.

Now she takes the thermometer out of her mouth, looks at it, smiles, everything is all right, and puts it away in a little lilac carrying case.

The sailor does not understand what the captain said, so the captain has to repeat it.

A STUDY IN
CALIFORNIA FLOWERS

OH, suddenly it's nothing to see on the way and it's nothing when I get there, and I'm in a coffeehouse, listening to a woman talk who's wearing more clothes than I have money in the world.

She is adorned in yellow and jewelry and a language that I cannot understand. She is talking about something that is of no importance, insisting on it. I can tell all this because the man who is with her will buy none of it, and stares absent-mindedly at the universe.

The man has not spoken a word since they sat down here with cups of espresso coffee accompanying them like small black dogs. Perhaps he does not care to speak any more. I think he is her husband.

Suddenly she breaks into English. She says, "He should know. They're his flowers," in the only language I understand and there's no reply echoing all the way back to the beginning where nothing could ever have been any different.

I was born forever to chronicle this: I don't know these people and they aren't my flowers.

THE BETRAYED KINGDOM

THIS love story took place during the last spring of the Beat Generation. She must be in her middle thirties and I wonder what she's doing now and if she still goes to parties.

Her name slips my memory. It has joined all the other names that I have forgotten that swirl through my head like a tide pool of discontinued faces and invisible syllables.

She lived in Berkeley and I saw her often at the parties I attended that spring.

She'd come to a party all sexied up and really move it around and drink wine and flirt until midnight came and then she'd lay her scene on whomever was trying to get into her pants, which happened to be a lot of my friends who had cars. One after another they answered the fate that she had waiting for them.

"Is anyone driving to Berkeley? I need a ride to Berkeley," she would always announce erotically. She wore a little gold watch to keep track of the midnight.

One of my friends would always say yes behind too much

wine and drive her to Berkeley and she'd let them into her little apartment and then tell them that she wouldn't go to bed with them, that she didn't sleep with anybody, but if they wanted to, they could sleep on her floor. She had an extra wool blanket.

My friends would always be too drunk to drive back to San Francisco, so they would sleep on her floor, curled around that green army blanket and wake up in the morning, stiff and grouchy as a coyote with rheumatism. Neither coffee nor breakfast was ever offered and she had gotten another ride to Berkeley.

A few weeks later you'd see her at another party and come the midnight she'd sing her little song, "Is anybody driving to Berkeley? I need a ride to Berkeley." And some poor son-of-a-bitch, always one of my friends, would fall for it and keep an appointment with that blanket on her floor.

Obviously, I was never able to understand the attraction that existed for her because she did nothing to me. Of course, I didn't have a car. That was probably it. You had to have a car to understand her charms.

I remember one evening when everybody was drinking wine and having a good time, listening to music. Oh, those Beat Generation days! talking, wine and jazz!

Miss Berkeley Floor was drifting through the place spreading joy wherever she went, except among those friends of mine who had already availed themselves of her hospitality.

Then midnight came! and, "Is anybody driving to Berkeley." She always used the same words. I guess because they worked so well: perfectly.

A friend of mine who had told me of his adventures with her looked at me and smiled as another friend, a virgin to the experience and quite aroused behind an evening's wine, took the hook.

"I'll give you a ride home," he said.

"Wonderful," she said with a sexy smile.

"I hope he enjoys sleeping on the floor," my friend half-whispered to me, loud enough for her to hear but not quite loud enough for him to hear because he was kismeted to make an acquaintance with a Berkeley floor.

In other words, this girl's scene had become a *very* in-joke among the stung and they were always amused to see somebody else take that carnival ride to Berkeley.

She went and got her coat and out they traipsed but she had drunk a little too much wine herself and she got sick when they got to his car and she puked all over his front fender.

After she had emptied her stomach and was feeling a little better, my friend drove her to Berkeley and she made him sleep on the floor wrapped up in that God-damn blanket.

He came back to San Francisco the next morning: stiff, hung over and so fucking mad at her that he never washed her puke off that fender. He drove around San Francisco for months with that stuff residing there like a betrayed kingdom until it wore itself away.

This might have been a funny story if it weren't for the fact that people need a little loving and, God, sometimes it's sad all the shit they have to go through to find some.

WOMEN WHEN THEY
PUT THEIR CLOTHES ON
IN THE MORNING

IT'S really a very beautiful exchange of values when women put their clothes on in the morning and she is brand-new and you've never seen her put her clothes on before.

You've been lovers and you've slept together and there's nothing more you can do about that, so it's time for her to put her clothes on.

Maybe you've already had breakfast and she's slipped her sweater on to cook a nice bare-assed breakfast for you, padding in sweet flesh around the kitchen, and you both discussed in length the poetry of Rilke which she knew a great deal about, surprising you.

But now it's time for her to put her clothes on because you've both had so much coffee that you can't drink any more and it's time for her to go home and it's time for her to go to work and you want to stay there alone because you've got some things to do around the house and you're going outside together for a nice walk and it's time for *you* to go home and it's time for *you* to go to work and she's got some things that she wants to do around the house.

Or . . . maybe it's even love.

But anyway: It's time for her to put her clothes on and it's so beautiful when she does it. Her body slowly disappears and comes out quite nicely all in clothes. There's a virginal quality to it. She's got her clothes on, and the beginning is over.

HALLOWEEN
IN DENVER

SHE didn't think that she would get any trick or treaters, so she didn't buy anything for them. That seems simple enough, doesn't it? Well, let's see what can happen with that. It might be interesting.

We'll start off with me reacting to her diagnosis of the situation by saying, "Hell, get something for the kids. After all, you're living on Telegraph Hill and there are a lot of kids in the neighborhood and some of them are certain to stop here."

I said it in such a way that she went down to the store and came back a few minutes later with a carton of gum. The gum was in little boxes called Chiclets and there were a lot of them in the carton.

"Satisfied?" she said.

She's an Aries.

"Yes," I said.

I'm an Aquarius.

We also had two pumpkins: both Scorpios.

So I sat there at the kitchen table and carved a pumpkin. It was the first pumpkin that I had carved in many years. It was kind of fun. My pumpkin had one round eye and one triangular eye and a not-very-bright witchy smile.

She cooked a wonderful dinner of sweet red cabbage and sausages and had some apples baking in the oven.

Then she carved her pumpkin while dinner was cooking beautifully away. Her pumpkin looked very modernistic when she was through. It looked more like an appliance than a jack-o'-lantern.

All the time that we were carving pumpkins the door bell did not ring once. It was completely empty of trick or treaters, but I did not panic, though there were an awful lot of Chiclets waiting anxiously in a large bowl.

We had dinner at 7:30 and it was so good. Then the meal was eaten and there were still no trick or treaters and it was after eight and things were starting to look bad. I was getting nervous.

I began to think that it was every day except Halloween.

She of course looked beatifically down upon the scene with an aura of Buddhistic innocence and carefully did not mention the fact that no trick or treaters had darkened the door.

That did not make things any better.

At nine o'clock we went in and lay down upon her bed and we were talking about this and that and I was in a kind of outrage because we had been forsaken by all trick or treaters, and I said something like, "Where are those little bastards?"

I had moved the bowl of Chiclets into the bedroom, so I could get to the trick or treaters faster when the door bell rang. The bowl sat there despondently on a table beside the bed. It was a very lonely sight.

At 9:30 we started fucking.

About fifty-four seconds later we heard a band of kids come running up the stairs accompanied by a cyclone of Halloween shrieking and mad door bell ringing.

I looked down at her and she looked up at me and our eyes met in laughter, but it wasn't too loud because suddenly we weren't at home.

We were in Denver, holding hands at a street corner, waiting for the light to change.

ATLANTISBURG

THERE were a couple of pool tables in the back and a table full of drunks nearby. I was talking to a young man who'd just gotten fired from his job and he was happy about it, but bored with the evening and the thought of looking for work next week. He was also quite disturbed about his home situation and went into it at great length.

We talked for a while, both of us leaning up against a pinball machine. There was a game of pool going on in the back. A little black Lesbian with a bull cut to her was playing pool with an old Italian, a sort of working type. Maybe he worked with vegetables or he was something else. The Lesbian was a seaman. They were locked in their game.

One of the drunks at the table spilled his drink all over the table and all over himself.

"Get a bar rag," another drunk said.

The spiller got up unevenly and went over to the bar and asked the bartender for a rag. The bartender leaned over the bar and said something to him that we couldn't hear.

The drunk came back and sat down. He did not have a bar rag.

"Where's the rag?" the other drunk said.

"He said I owe him forty-five dollars and sixty cents. My tab . . ."

"Well, I don't owe him forty-five dollars and sixty cents. I'll go over and get a bar rag. This table is a mess," and gets up to prove that he doesn't owe the bartender forty-five dollars and sixty cents.

The table was returned to normal. They started talking about something that I know about.

Finally my friend said, "What a God-damn boring night. I think I'll watch that dike play pool."

"I think I'll stay here and listen to these drunks for a while," I said.

He walked over and watched the black Lesbian play pool with the old Italian. I stood there leaning up against the pinball machine, listening to the drunks talk about lost cities.

THE VIEW FROM
THE DOG TOWER

". . . three German shepherd puppies wandered away from their home up near the County line."

—*North County Journal*
Serving Northern Santa Cruz County

I have been thinking about this little item that I read in the *North County Journal* for a couple of months now. It contains the boundaries of a small tragedy. I know we are surrounded by so much blossoming horror in the world (Vietnam, starvation, rioting, living in hopeless fear, etc.) that three puppies wandering off isn't very much, but I worry about it and see this simple event as the possible telescope for a larger agony.

". . . three German shepherd puppies wandered away from their home up near the County line." It sounds like something from a Bob Dylan song.

Perhaps they vanished playing, barking and chasing each other, into the woods where lost they are to this very day, cringing around like scraps of dogs, looking for any small thing to eat, intellectually unable to comprehend what has happened to them because their brains are welded to their stomachs.

Their voices are used now only to cry out in fear and hunger, and all their playing days are over, those days of careless pleasure that led them into the terrible woods.

I fear that these poor lost dogs may be the shadow of a future journey if we don't watch out.

GREYHOUND TRAGEDY

SHE wanted her life to be a movie magazine tragedy like the death of a young star with long lines of people weeping and a corpse more beautiful than a great painting, but she was never able to leave the small Oregon town that she was born and raised in and go to Hollywood and die.

Though it was the Depression, her life was comfortable and untouched because her father was the manager of the local Penney's and financially compassionate to his family.

Movies were the religion of her life and she attended every service with a bag of popcorn. Movie magazines were her Bible that she studied with the zealousness of a doctor of divinity. She probably knew more about movies than the Pope.

The years passed like the subscriptions to her magazines: 1931, 1932, 1933, 1934, 1935, 1936, 1937, until September 2, 1938.

Finally it was time to make her move if she were ever going to go to Hollywood. There was a young man who wanted to marry her. Her parents were very enthusiastic about his prospects. They approved of him because he was a Ford salesman. "It's a company with a fine tradition," her father said. Things did not look good for her.

She spent months building up the courage to go down to the bus station to find out how much the fare to Hollywood cost. Sometimes she spent whole days thinking about the bus station. A few times she even got dizzy and had to sit down. It never dawned on her that she could have called on the telephone.

She made it a point during those nervous months never to go by the bus station. Thinking about it all the time was one thing but actually seeing it was another.

Once she was driving downtown with her mother and her mother turned onto the street where the bus station was located and she asked her mother to *please* turn down another street because she wanted to buy something at a store on that street.

Some shoes.

Her mother thought nothing of it and made the turn. She didn't think to ask her daughter why her face was red but that was not unusual because she seldom thought to ask her anything.

One morning she was going to talk to her about all the movie magazines that came in the mail. Some days they would jam up the mailbox, so that she would have to use a screwdriver to get the mail out. But her mother had forgotten about it by noon. Her mother's memory had never been able to last until twelve. It usually pooped out around 11:30, but she was a good cook if the recipes were simple.

Time was running out like the popcorn at a Clark Gable picture. Her father had been dropping a lot of "hints" lately about her being out of high school for three years and perhaps it was time for her to think about doing something with her life.

He was not the local manager of Penney's for nothing. Recently, actually about a year ago, he had become tired of watching his daughter sit around the house all the time reading movie magazines with her eyes wide as saucers. He had begun to think of her as a bump on a log.

Her father's hints happened to coincide with the young Ford salesman's fourth proposal of marriage. She had turned down the other three saying that she needed time to think it over which really meant that she was trying to build up enough courage to go down to the bus station and find out what the fare to Hollywood cost.

At last the pressure of her own longings and her father's "hints" made her leave the house early one warm twilight, after getting out of doing the dinner dishes, and walk slowly down to the bus station. From March 10, 1938 until the evening of September 2, 1938, she had been wondering what a bus ticket to Hollywood cost.

The bus station was stark, unromantic and very distant from the silver screen. Two old people were sitting there on a bench waiting for a bus. The old people were tired. They wanted to be now at wherever they were going. Their suitcase was like a burned-out light bulb.

The man who sold the tickets looked as if he could have sold anything. He could just as well be selling washing machines or lawn furniture as tickets to other places.

She was red-faced and nervous. Her heart felt out of place in the bus station. She tried to act as if she were waiting for somebody to come in on the next bus, an aunt, as she worked desperately to build up enough courage to go ask how much it cost to go to Hollywood but it didn't make any difference to anybody else what games she pretended.

Nobody looked at her, though she could have rented herself out as an earthquake beet. They simply didn't care. It was a stupid night in September and she just didn't have enough nerve to find out how much the fare to Hollywood cost.

She cried all the way home through the warm gentle Oregon night, wanting to die every time her feet touched the ground. There was no wind and all the shadows were comforting. They were like cousins to her, so she married the young Ford salesman and drove a new car every year except for the Second World War.

She had two children that she named Jean and Rudolph and tried to let her beautiful movie star death go at that, but now, thirty-one years later, she still blushes when she passes the bus station.

CRAZY OLD WOMEN
ARE RIDING THE BUSES
OF AMERICA TODAY
For Marcia Pacaud

THERE is one of them sitting behind me right now. She is wearing an old hat that's got plastic fruit on it, and her eyes dart back and forth across her face like fruit flies.

The man sitting next to her is pretending that he is dead.

The crazy old woman talks to him in one continuous audio breath that passes out of her mouth like a vision of angry bowling alleys on Saturday night with millions of pins crashing off her teeth.

The man sitting next to her is an old, very little Chinese man and he's wearing the clothes of a teen-ager. His coat, pants, shoes and cap belong to a fifteen-year-old boy. I've seen a lot of old Chinese men wearing teen-age clothes. It must be strange when they go to the store and buy them.

The Chinese man has scrunched himself up next to the window, and you can't even tell he's breathing. She doesn't care if he's dead or alive.

He was alive before she sat down beside him and started telling him about her children that came to no good and her husband who is an alcoholic and the leak in the God-damn car roof that he won't fix because he's always drunk, the son-of-a-bitch, and she's too tired to do anything because she works all the time at a cafe, I must be the oldest waitress in the world, and her feet can't take it any more and her son's in the penitentiary and her daughter is living with an alcoholic truck driver and they've got three little bastards running around the house and she wishes she had a television because she can't listen to the radio any more.

She stopped listening to the radio ten years ago because she couldn't find any programs on it. All there is is music and news now and I don't like the music and I can't understand the news and she doesn't care if this fucking Chinaman is alive or dead.

She ate some Chinese food twenty-three years ago in Sacramento and crapped for five days afterwards and all she can see is one ear facing her mouth.

The ear looks like a little yellow dead horn.

THE CORRECT TIME

I'LL do a bubble the best I can and perhaps a few more. Not that they are overly important and would change things, except for the one that got hit by the Number 30 Stockton bus. That's another story.

My girlfriend was late, so I went to the park alone. I got tired of waiting, of standing there in a bookstore reading a novel about people who make love all the time in wealthy surroundings. She was good-looking, but I was also growing older, jaded.

It was one of those typical summer afternoons that we do not get in San Francisco until the autumn. The park was as usual: Children were playing these-are-the-days-of-my-youth, and old people were sunning now what the grave would darken soon enough and the beatniks were lying here and there like stale rugs on the grass, waiting for the great hip rug merchant to come along.

I walked all around the park before I sat down: a long slow circle gathered gently to its end. Then I sat down but before I could examine the territory of where I was at, an old man asked me what time it was.

"A quarter of three," I said, though I did not know what time it was. I just wanted to be helpful.

"Thank you," he said, and flashed an antique smile of relief.

A quarter of three was the correct time for that old man for that was the time he wanted, the time that pleased him the most. I felt pretty good.

I sat there for a few moments and saw nothing else to remember and nothing to forget. I got up and went away, leaving a happy old man behind.

The Boy Scouts of America taught me all I know, and I had done my good deed for the day, and all I needed now so that I could dwell in perfection would be to find an enfeebled fire engine and help it across the street.

"Thank you, son," with its arthritic red paint smelling of old age, and its ladder covered with white hair, and a slight cataract over its siren.

There were children playing a game with bubbles at the place I had chosen to leave the park. They had a jar of magic bubble stuff and little rods with metal rings to cast the bubbles away with, to join them with the air.

Instead of leaving the park, I stood and watched the bubbles leave the park. They had a very high mortality pulse. I saw them again and again suddenly die above the sidewalk and the street: their rainbow profiles ceasing to exist.

I wondered what was happening and then looked closer to see that they were colliding with insects in the air. What a lovely idea! and then one of the bubbles was hit by the Number 30 Stockton bus.

WHAM! like the collision between an inspired trumpet and a great concerto, and showed all those other bubbles how to go out in the grand style.

HOLIDAY IN GERMANY

LET'S put it up front right now: I'm not an expert on holidays. I just don't have that kind of money. You might even go so far as to say that I am poor. I don't mind because it's true.

I am thirty, and my average income has been around $1400 a year for the last ten years. America is a very wealthy country, so sometimes I feel anti-American. I mean, I feel as if I am letting America down because I'm not making enough money to justify my citizenship.

Anyway, it's hard to holiday on $1400 a year and yesterday I was taking the Greyhound bus to Monterey to stay for a couple of weeks as a kind of exile from San Francisco.

I won't go into the reasons why. I am afraid that too much humor would ruin this story because actually it has very little to do with me. I just went along for the ride.

It concerns the two German boys that were on the bus. They were in their early twenties and sitting in the seat in front of me. They were in America for a three-week vacation. It was almost over: too bad.

They were yakking it up in German and touristing away, pointing out this and that as the bus rolled toward Monterey.

The German boy sitting next to the window also had a deep interest in the contents of American automobiles, especially the female contents. Whenever he would spot a good-looking girl driving along, he would point her out to his friend as part of their itinerary in America.

They were healthy, normal sex fiends.

A Volkswagen sedan came by the German boy on the window and he immediately got his friend's attention by pointing out two good-looking young girls in the Volkswagen. The German boys really had their faces pressed against the window now.

The girl on the passenger side, she was right beneath us, had short blond hair and a gentle white neck. The Volkswagen and the bus were travelling at the same rate of speed.

As the German boys continued to stare down at her, she grew kind of nervous, self-conscious, but she did not know why this was happening because she couldn't see us. She was now playing with her hair as women are prone to do under such conditions, even if they don't know quite what's up.

The lane of traffic in front of the Volkswagen slowed down and our bus went roaring ahead of the car. We were gone from each other for about a minute when the Volkswagen came up on us again.

The German boys picked up on this instantly and their faces were pressed against the window, participating in the age-old Candy-Store-Sex-Window Syndrome.

This time the girl looked up and saw the German boys staring down, all big smiles and flirting. The girl returned a kind of ambiguous half-smile. She was a perfect freeway Mona Lisa.

We hit another scramble of traffic and the Volkswagen

suffered from it and fell back, but a couple of minutes later it was up with us again. We were both moving about sixty miles an hour.

This time when she of the blond hair, the gentle white neck looked up and saw the German boys flirting away, she gave them a great big smile and waved enthusiastically. They had shattered her cool.

The German boys were waving like a convention of flags with mile-a-minute flirting and smiling. They were very happy: Ah, America!

The girl had a lovely smile. Her friend waved, too, driving the Volkswagen with one hand. She was also a good-looking girl: another blonde, but with long hair.

The German boys were having a fine holiday in America. Too bad there was no way they could get out of that bus and into the Volkswagen to meet the girls, but things like that are impossible.

Soon the girls took an off ramp to Palo Alto and disappeared forever, not unless of course, they take a holiday next year in Germany and are driving along the autobahn in a bus.

SAND CASTLES

STRANGE fences grow on Point Reyes Peninsula which is fastened like a haunted fingerprint to the California coast. Odd perspectives are constantly drifting out of sight or becoming too intimate in this place where white medieval Portuguese dairies suddenly appear cradled by cypress trees and then disappear as if they had never really been there at all.

Hawks circle in the sky like the lost springs of old railroad watches looking for correct protein wandering somewhere below to swoop down upon and devour chronologically.

It is not often that I journey to Point Reyes because, frankly, my mind is seldom in that place, but when I do go there I always enjoy myself. That is, if enjoy is the right word, driving down a road lined with fences that look like cemeteries lost in half-vague and half-mercuric spiritual density.

I usually end up going to a place called McClures Beach at the end of the peninsula. There's a parking lot where you leave your car and then it's a good hike down a gradual canyon to the beach, following a small creek.

Watercress grows luxuriously in the creek.

There are many peculiar flowers as step by step you disappear down into the turns of the canyon until at last you arrive at the Pacific Ocean and a dramatic beach like a photograph if they'd had cameras in the days when Christ lived, and now you are a part of the photograph, but sometimes you have to pinch yourself to make sure that you are really there.

I remember one afternoon many years ago I went with a friend to Point Reyes where my mind was exactly in that kind of place and stared at the fences as we drove deeper and deeper into the peninsula which of course unfolded like layers of abstraction and intimacy constantly being circled by hawks.

We parked at McClures Beach. I remember very clearly the sound of the car being parked. It made a lot of noise. There were some other cars parked there. Even after our car was parked, totally silent, it was still making noise.

Warm fog swirled in the canyon as we gradually descended. A hundred feet in front of us everything was lost in the fog and a hundred feet behind us everything was lost in the fog. We were walking in a capsule between amnesias.

There were hushed flowers all around us. The flowers looked as if they had been painted by a Fourteenth Century anonymous French painter. My friend and I had not said anything to each other for a long time. Perhaps our tongues had joined the brushes of that painter.

I stared at the watercress in the creek. It looked wealthy. Whenever I see watercress, which isn't very often, I think of the rich. I think they are the only people who can afford it and they use watercress in exotic recipes that they keep hidden in vaults from the poor.

Suddenly we went around a turn in the canyon and there were five handsome teen-age boys in swimming suits burying five pretty teen-age girls in the sand. They were all carved from classical California physical marble.

The girls had arrived at various stages of being buried. One of them was completely buried with only her head above the sand. She was very beautiful with long black hair stretched out along the sand as if it were some kind of dark water, perhaps jade, flowing out of her head.

The girls were all very happy being buried in the sand and so were the boys who were burying them in the sand. It was a teen-age graveyard party because they had run out of everything else to do. They were surrounded by towels, beer cans, beach baskets, picnic leftovers, etc.

They gave us no particular attention as we walked by and down to the Pacific Ocean where I mentally pinched myself to make sure that I was still in this Christ-powered photograph.

FORGIVEN

THIS story is a close friend or perhaps even a lover to a story called "Elmira." They both deal in a way with the Long Tom River and the time when I was young, a teen-ager, and somehow the Long Tom River was a part of my spiritual DNA.

I really needed that river. It was the beginning answers to some very complicated questions in my life that I am still trying to work out.

I'm quite aware that Richard Brautigan has written a novel called *Trout Fishing in America* that deals thoroughly with trout fishing and its kaleidoscope of environments, so I'm a little embarrassed to try something in the same theme, but I'm going to go ahead because this is a story that I have to tell.

I used to go fishing on the Long Tom River way back in the mountains where the river in parts wasn't much wider than a coffee table with a best seller sitting on it.

The trout were little cutthroats between six and ten inches long and a lot of fun to catch. I really got good at fishing the Long Tom and could take my limit of ten fish in little over an hour if I had any kind of luck at all.

The Long Tom River was forty miles away. I usually hitch-hiked there late in the afternoon and would leave in the twilight to hitch-hike the forty miles back home.

A few times I hitch-hiked there in the rain and fished in the rain and hitch-hiked back in the rain. I travelled eighty miles in a wet circle.

I'd get out at a bridge across the Long Tom and fish down half a mile to another bridge across the river. It was a wooden bridge that looked like an angel. The river was sort of murky. It was gentle fishing between the bridges, down through a lazy dripping landscape.

Below the second bridge, which looked like a white wooden angel, the Long Tom River flowed into very strange ways. It was dark and haunting and went something like this: Every hundred yards or so there was a large open swamp-like pool and then the river flowed out of the pool into a fast shallow run covered over closely with trees like a shadowy knitted tunnel until it reached the next swampy pool and very seldom did I let the Long Tom River call me down into there.

But late one August afternoon I had fished down to the angel bridge and the fishing hadn't been very good. I only had four or five trout.

It was raining and very warm up there in the mountains and edging toward sundown and actually it may have been early twilight. I couldn't tell exactly what time it was because of the rain.

Anyway: I was taken by some goofy kid reason to try a little fishing down below the bridge into those knitted river tunnels and big swampy open pools.

It was really too late to go down into there and I should have just turned around and got out of there and hitch-hiked the forty miles back home through the rain.

I should have let well enough alone.

But, Oh no, I started fishing down into there. It was tropical in the tunnels and I was catching trout where the tunnels flowed into the big swampy pools. Then I'd have to wade around the pools through deep warm mud.

I lost a trout that went about thirteen inches long and that really got my excitement up, so I continued fishing down further and further until I was six swampy pools past the wooden angel bridge when suddenly, out of nowhere, the light just dropped away within a few moments, falling into total night and there I was halfway around the sixth swampy pool in the dark, and in front of me there was nothing but darkness and water, and behind me was nothing but darkness and water.

The strangest God-damn feeling of fear shook through me. It was just like a crystal chandelier made out of adrenaline swaying wildly in an earthquake, and I turned around and fled up the river, splashing like an alligator around the big swampy pools and running like a dog up the shallow tunnels.

Every horror in the world was at my back, at my sides and directly in front of me and they were all without names and had no shape but perception itself.

When at last I ran out of the final tunnel and saw the dim white outline of the bridge standing out against the night, my soul was born again through a vision of rescue and sanctuary.

As I got closer and closer, the bridge bloomed like a white wooden angel in my eyes until I was sitting on the bridge, resting and soaking wet but not at all cold in the constant rain of the mountain evening.

I hope that Richard Brautigan will forgive me for writing this story.

AMERICAN FLAG DECAL

THIS story begins with an American flag decal on the rear window of a pickup truck, but you can barely see it because the truck is far away and then it turns off the highway onto a side road and it's gone, but somehow we have started again.

It's good to be back in California after a very unhappy month in the East: New York, etc. . . . with too much drunkenness, days and days of cold autumn rain and love affairs that were breathing mirrors of my unhappiness.

Now out here driving through the California countryside with a friend all we have to do is find somebody to repair his broken cesspool. It's a mess. We need somebody right now whose living is made from the knowing and handling of cesspools.

We drive down one road and then another, looking for a particular cesspool man. We stop at a place where we think he lives, but we are very wrong by about a million miles. It's a place that sells honey.

We don't know how we made the mistake. It's a long ways

from a cesspool man to some women behind a screen door selling honey.

We think it's amusing and so do they. We laugh at ourselves and they laugh at us. We are funny and drive away talking about the inner and outer roads that a man travels down to arrive at owning a grocery store or being a doctor or knowing cesspools intimately or how somebody else decides to sell honey but then is mistaken for a cesspool man.

A short, humorously spiritual distance away we find a cesspool man who's at home surrounded by all the equipment that he needs to successfully exercise cesspools.

Three men are fixing a broken truck. They stop working and turn to look at us. They are very serious in a country-casual way.

"No, not today. We got to fix this truck, so we can go bear hunting."

And that's it and there you have it: They want to fix the truck, so they can go bear hunting. Our cesspool is transparent, child-like. Bears are more important. I'm glad to be back in California.

THE WORLD WAR I
LOS ANGELES AIRPLANE

HE was found lying dead near the television set on the front
room floor of a small rented house in Los Angeles. My wife
had gone to the store to get some ice cream. It was an early-
in-the-night-just-a-few-blocks-away store. We were in an ice-
cream mood. The telephone rang. It was her brother to say
that her father had died that afternoon. He was seventy. I
waited for her to come home with the ice cream. I tried to
think of the best way to tell her that her father was dead with
the least amount of pain but you cannot camouflage death
with words. Always at the end of the words somebody is dead.

She was very happy when she came back from the store.

"What's wrong?" she said.

"Your brother just called from Los Angeles," I said.

"What happened?" she said.

"Your father died this afternoon."

That was in 1960 and now it's just a few weeks away
from 1970. He has been dead for almost ten years and I've

done a lot of thinking about what his death means to all of us.

1. He was born from German blood and raised on a farm in South Dakota. His grandfather was a terrible tyrant who completely destroyed his three grown sons by treating them exactly the way he treated them when they were children. They never grew up in his eyes and they never grew up in their own eyes. He made sure of that. They never left the farm. They of course got married but he handled all of their domestic matters except for the siring of his grandchildren. He never allowed them to discipline their own children. He took care of that for them. Her father thought of his father as another brother who was always trying to escape the never-relenting wrath of their grandfather.

2. He was smart, so he became a schoolteacher when he was eighteen and he left the farm which was an act of revolution against his grandfather who from that day forth considered him dead. He didn't want to end up like his father, hiding behind the barn. He taught school for three years in the Midwest and then he worked as an automobile salesman in the pioneer days of car selling.

3. There was an early marriage followed by an early divorce with feelings afterward that left the marriage hanging like a skeleton in her family's closet because he tried to keep it a secret. He probably had been very much in love.

4. There was a horrible automobile accident just before the First World War in which everybody was killed except him. It was one of those automobile accidents that leave deep spiritual scars like historical landmarks on the family and friends of the dead.

5. When America went into the First World War in 1917, he decided that he wanted to be a pilot, though he was in his late twenties. He was told that it would be impossible because

he was too old but he projected so much energy into his desire to fly that he was accepted for pilot training and went to Florida and became a pilot.

In 1918 he went to France and flew a De Havilland and bombed a railroad station in France and one day he was flying over the German lines when little clouds began appearing around him and he thought that they were beautiful and flew for a long time before he realized that they were German antiaircraft guns trying to shoot him down.

Another time he was flying over France and a rainbow appeared behind the tail of his plane and every turn that the plane made, the rainbow also made the same turn and it followed after him through the skies of France for part of an afternoon in 1918.

6. When the war was over he got out a captain and he was travelling on a train through Texas when the middle-aged man sitting next to him and with whom he had been talking for about three hundred miles said, "If I was a young man like you and had a little extra cash, I'd go up to Idaho and start a bank. There's a good future in Idaho banking."

7. That's what her father did.

8. He went to Idaho and started a bank which soon led to three more banks and a large ranch. It was by now 1926 and everything was going all right.

9. He married a schoolteacher who was sixteen years his junior and for their honeymoon they took a train to Philadelphia and spent a week there.

10. When the stock market crashed in 1929 he was hit hard by it and had to give up his banks and a grocery store that he had picked up along the way, but he still had the ranch, though he had to put a mortgage on it.

11. He decided to go into sheep raising in 1931 and got a big flock and was very good to his sheepherders. He was so

good to them that it was a subject of gossip in his part of Idaho. The sheep got some kind of horrible sheep disease and all died.

12. He got another big flock of sheep in 1933 and added more fuel to the gossip by continuing to be so good to his men. The sheep got some kind of horrible sheep disease and all died in 1934.

13. He gave his men a big bonus and went out of the sheep business.

14. He had just enough money left over after selling the ranch to pay off all his debts and buy a brand-new Chevrolet which he put his family into and he drove off to California to start all over again.

15. He was forty-four, had a twenty-eight-year-old wife and an infant daughter.

16. He didn't know anyone in California and it was the Depression.

17. His wife worked for a while in a prune shed and he parked cars at a lot in Hollywood.

18. He got a job as a bookkeeper for a small construction company.

19. His wife gave birth to a son.

20. In 1940 he went briefly into California real estate, but then decided not to pursue it any further and went back to work for the construction company as a bookkeeper.

21. His wife got a job as a checker in a grocery store where she worked for eight years and then an assistant manager quit and opened his own store and she went to work for him and she still works there.

22. She has worked twenty-three years now as a grocery checker for the same store.

23. She was very pretty until she was forty.

24. The construction company laid him off. They said he

was too old to take care of the books. "It's time for you to go out to pasture," they joked. He was fifty-nine.

25. They rented the same house they lived in for twenty-five years, though they could have bought it at one time with no down payment and monthly payments of fifty dollars.

26. When his daughter was going to high school he was working there as the school janitor. She saw him in the halls. His working as a janitor was a subject that was very seldom discussed at home.

27. Her mother would make lunches for both of them.

28. He retired when he was sixty-five and became a very careful sweet wine alcoholic. He liked to drink whiskey but they couldn't afford to keep him in it. He stayed in the house most of the time and started drinking about ten o'clock, a few hours after his wife had gone off to work at the grocery store.

29. He would get quietly drunk during the course of the day. He always kept his wine bottles hidden in a kitchen cabinet and would secretly drink from them, though he was alone.

He very seldom made any bad scenes and the house was always clean when his wife got home from work. He did though after a while take on that meticulous manner of walking that alcoholics have when they are trying very carefully to act as if they aren't drunk.

30. He used sweet wine in place of life because he didn't have any more life to use.

31. He watched afternoon television.

32. Once he had been followed by a rainbow across the skies of France while flying a World War I airplane carrying bombs and machine guns.

33. "Your father died this afternoon."